Pokémon™ X•Y

STORY
Hidenori Kusaka

ART
Satoshi Yamamoto

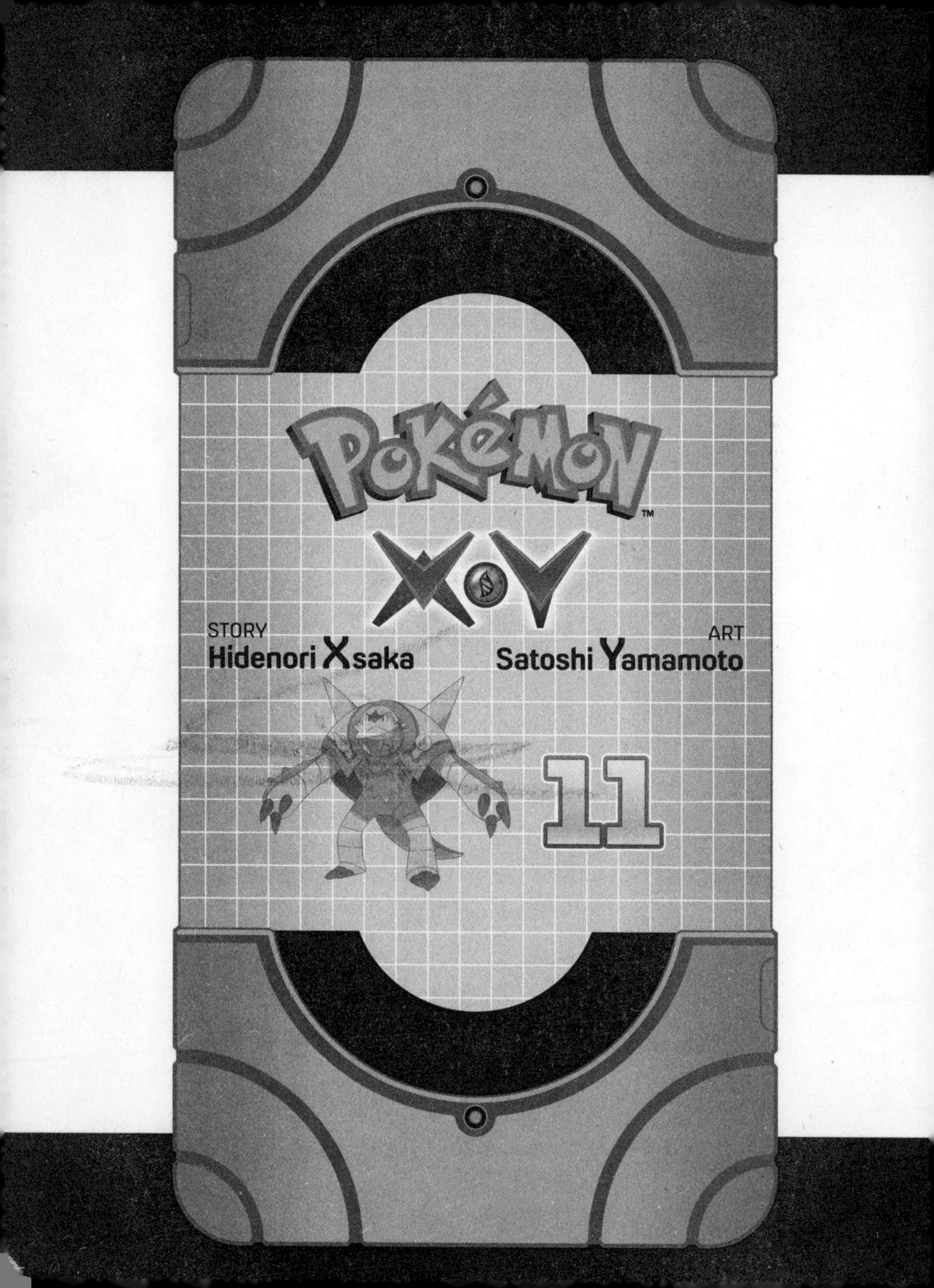

11

CHARACTERS

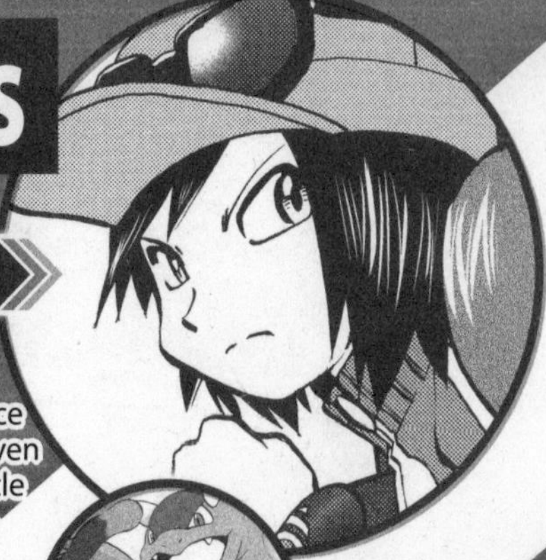

X

The main character of this chapter, and one of five close childhood friends. He was once a highly skilled Trainer who even won the Junior Pokémon Battle Tournament, but now...

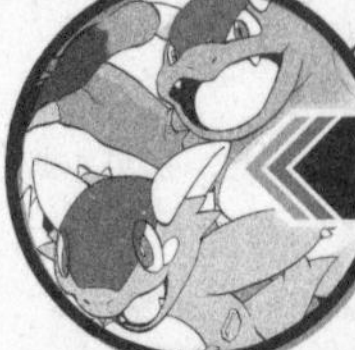

KANGA & LI'L KANGA

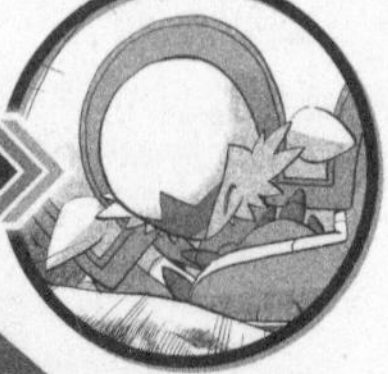

MARISSO

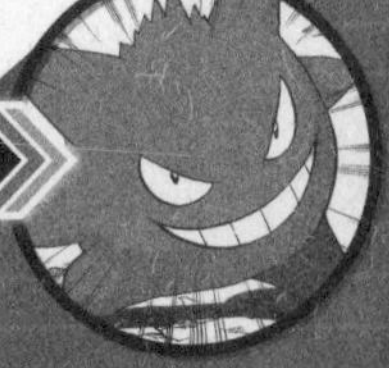

GARMA

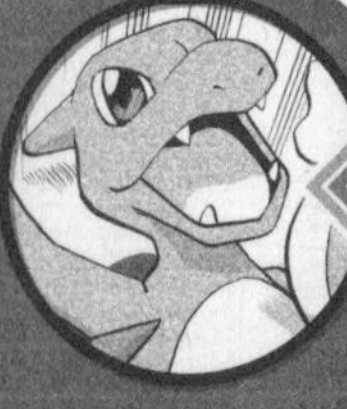

SALAMÈ

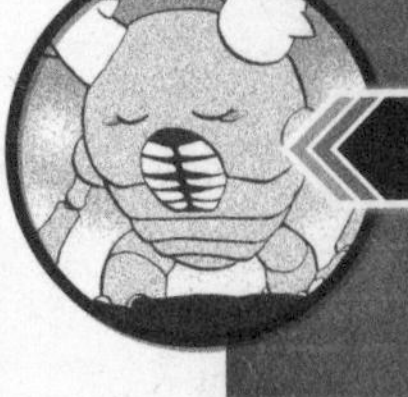

RUTE

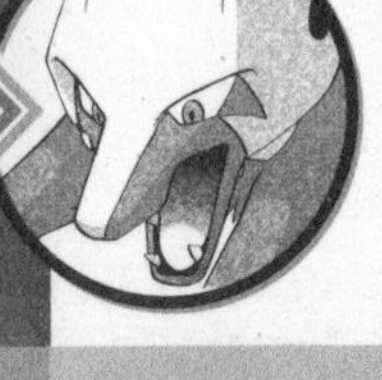

ÉLEC

OUR STORY THUS FAR...

In Vaniville Town in the Kalos region, X is a Pokémon Trainer child prodigy. But then he falls into a depression. A sudden attack by the Legendary Pokémon Xerneas and Yveltal, controlled by Team Flare, forces X out into the world. He and his closest childhood friends—Y, Trevor, Tierno and Shauna—are now on the run.

Y receives a Mega Ring and becomes a Mega Evolution successor. Then X and his friends learn the whereabouts of Team Flare's new hideout and head there for a showdown. But along the way they are ambushed by five scientists from Team Flare...!

MEET THE

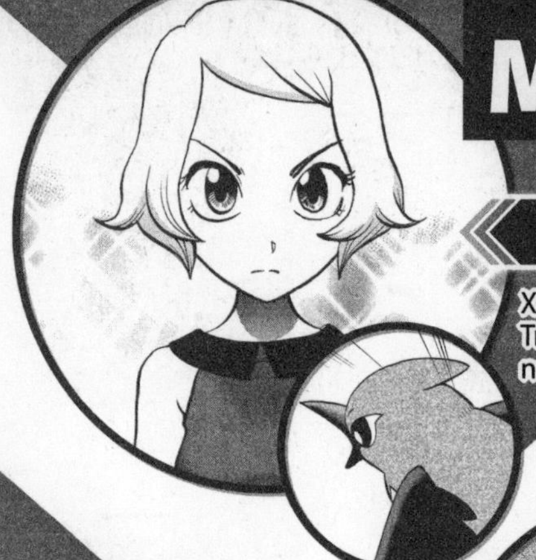

Y

X's best friend, a Sky Trainer trainee. Her full name is Yvonne Gabena.

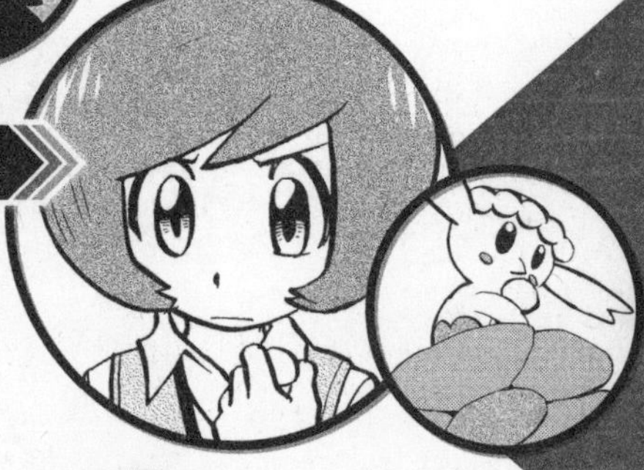

TREVOR

One of the five friends. A quiet boy who hopes to become a fine Pokémon Researcher one day.

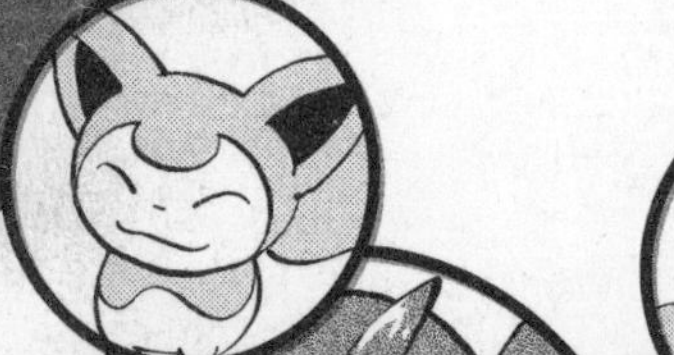

SHAUNA

One of the five friends. Her dream is to become a Furfrou Groomer. She is quick to speak her mind.

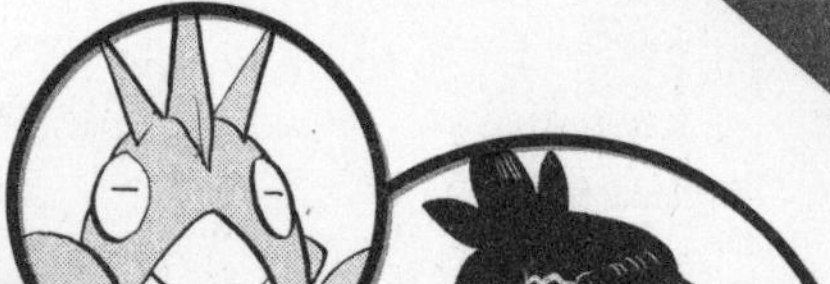

TIERNO

One of the five friends. A big boy with an even bigger heart. He is currently training to become a dancer.

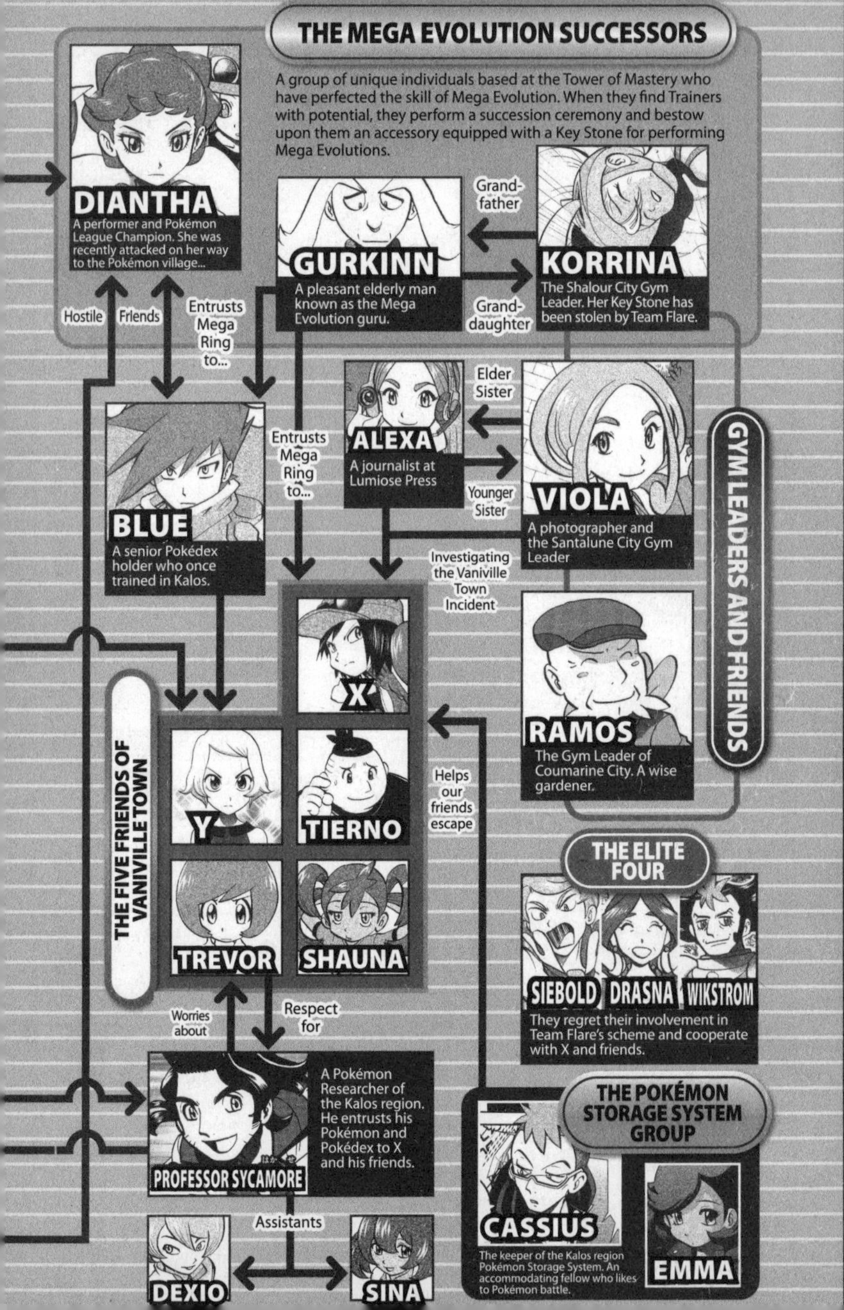

THE MEGA EVOLUTION SUCCESSORS
A group of unique individuals based at the Tower of Mastery who have perfected the skill of Mega Evolution. When they find Trainers with potential, they perform a succession ceremony and bestow upon them an accessory equipped with a Key Stone for performing Mega Evolutions.
DIANTHA
A performer and Pokémon League Champion. She was recently attacked on her way to the Pokémon village...
GURKINN
A pleasant elderly man known as the Mega Evolution guru.
KORRINA
The Shalour City Gym Leader. Her Key Stone has been stolen by Team Flare.
Grand-father
Grand-daughter
Hostile
Friends
Entrusts Mega Ring to...
GYM LEADERS AND FRIENDS
ALEXA
A journalist at Lumiose Press
VIOLA
A photographer and the Santalune City Gym Leader
Elder Sister
Younger Sister
BLUE
A senior Pokédex holder who once trained in Kalos.
Entrusts Mega Ring to...
Investigating the Vaniville Town Incident
RAMOS
The Gym Leader of Coumarine City. A wise gardener.
THE FIVE FRIENDS OF VANIVILLE TOWN
X
Y
TIERNO
TREVOR
SHAUNA
Helps our friends escape
THE ELITE FOUR
SIEBOLD
DRASNA
WIKSTROM
They regret their involvement in Team Flare's scheme and cooperate with X and friends.
Worries about
Respect for
PROFESSOR SYCAMORE
A Pokémon Researcher of the Kalos region. He entrusts his Pokémon and Pokédex to X and his friends.
Assistants
DEXIO
SINA
THE POKÉMON STORAGE SYSTEM GROUP
CASSIUS
The keeper of the Kalos region Pokémon Storage System. An accommodating fellow who likes to Pokémon battle.
EMMA

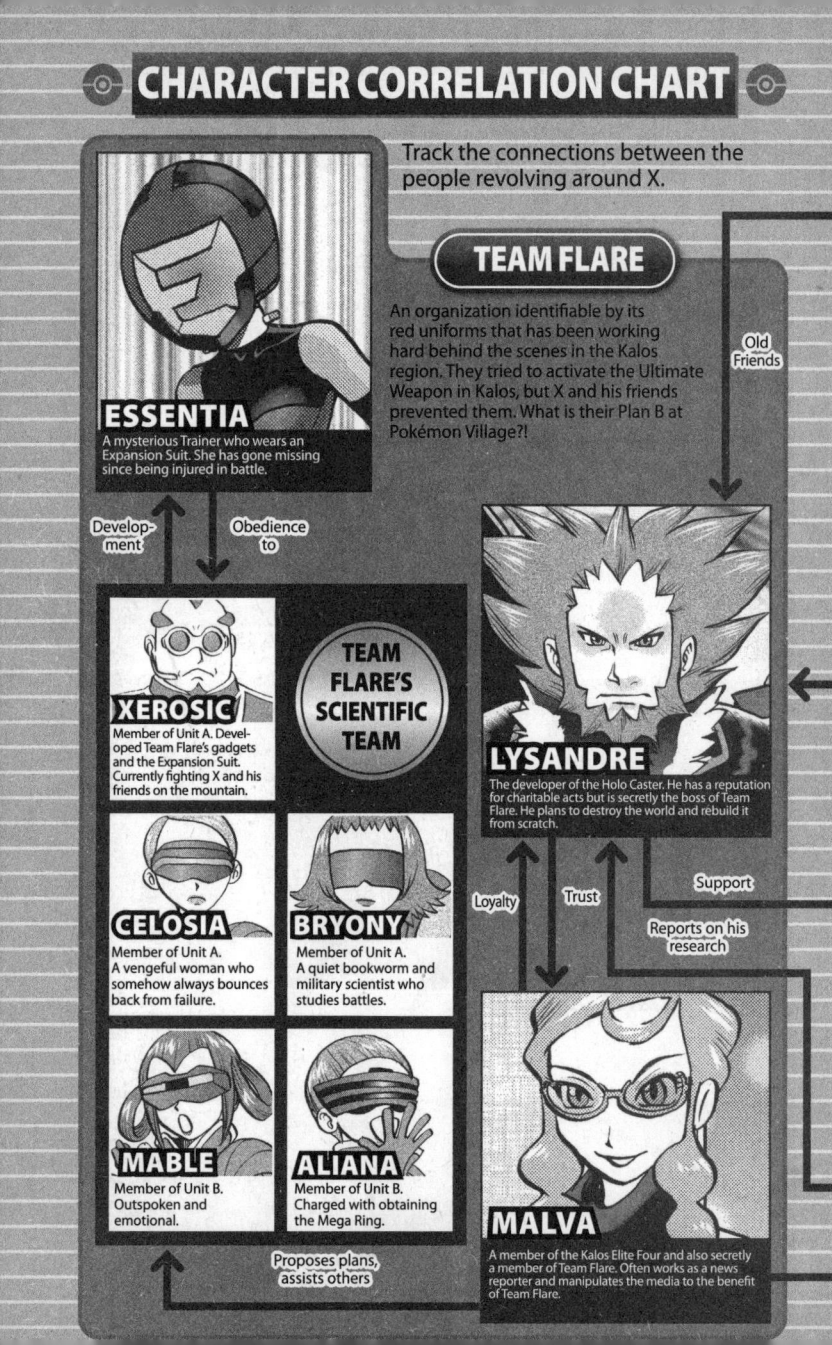

CHARACTER CORRELATION CHART

Track the connections between the people revolving around X.

ESSENTIA
A mysterious Trainer who wears an Expansion Suit. She has gone missing since being injured in battle.

TEAM FLARE
An organization identifiable by its red uniforms that has been working hard behind the scenes in the Kalos region. They tried to activate the Ultimate Weapon in Kalos, but X and his friends prevented them. What is their Plan B at Pokémon Village?!

Old Friends

Development

Obedience to

TEAM FLARE'S SCIENTIFIC TEAM

XEROSIC
Member of Unit A. Developed Team Flare's gadgets and the Expansion Suit. Currently fighting X and his friends on the mountain.

LYSANDRE
The developer of the Holo Caster. He has a reputation for charitable acts but is secretly the boss of Team Flare. He plans to destroy the world and rebuild it from scratch.

CELOSIA
Member of Unit A. A vengeful woman who somehow always bounces back from failure.

BRYONY
Member of Unit A. A quiet bookworm and military scientist who studies battles.

Loyalty

Trust

Support

Reports on his research

MABLE
Member of Unit B. Outspoken and emotional.

ALIANA
Member of Unit B. Charged with obtaining the Mega Ring.

MALVA
A member of the Kalos Elite Four and also secretly a member of Team Flare. Often works as a news reporter and manipulates the media to the benefit of Team Flare.

Proposes plans, assists others

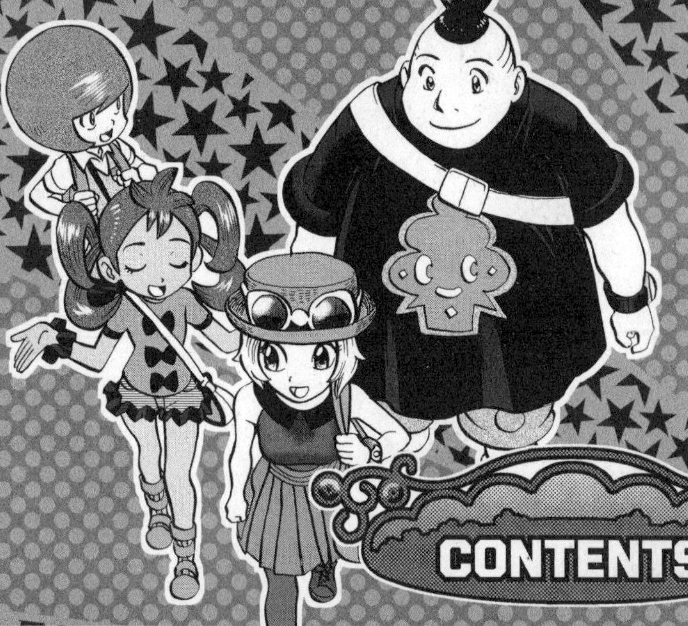

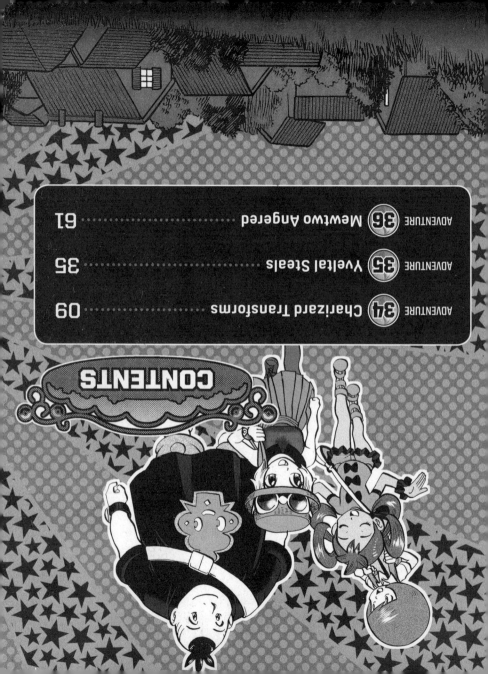

CONTENTS

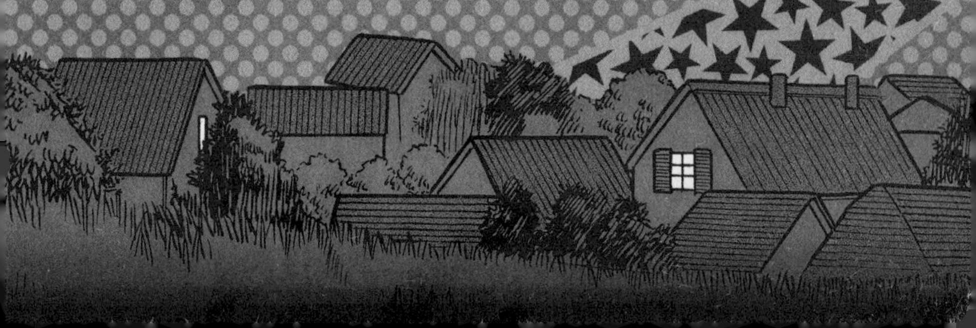

Adventure 34 Charizard Transforms

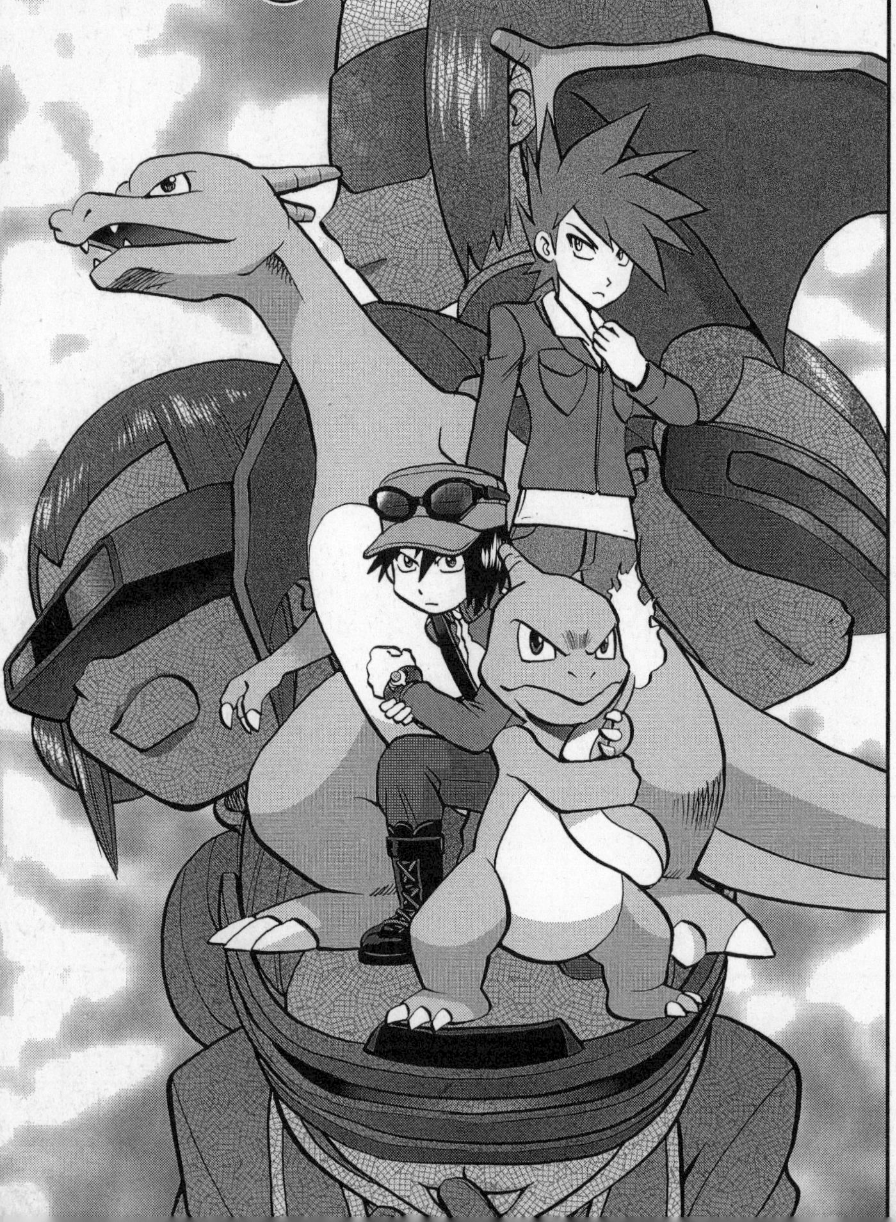

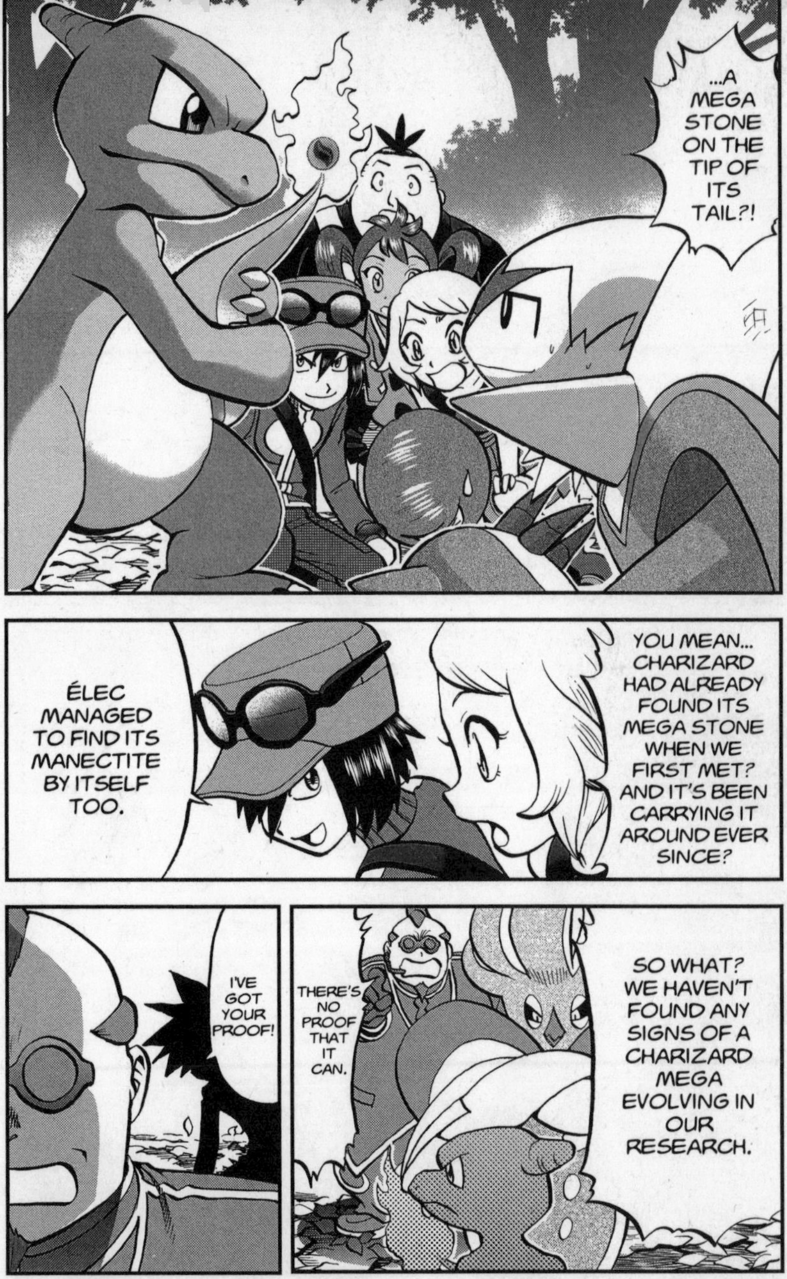
...A MEGA STONE ON THE TIP OF ITS TAIL?!
YOU MEAN... CHARIZARD HAD ALREADY FOUND ITS MEGA STONE WHEN WE FIRST MET? AND IT'S BEEN CARRYING IT AROUND EVER SINCE?
ÉLEC MANAGED TO FIND ITS MANECTITE BY ITSELF TOO.
SO WHAT? WE HAVEN'T FOUND ANY SIGNS OF A CHARIZARD MEGA EVOLVING IN OUR RESEARCH.
THERE'S NO PROOF THAT IT CAN.
I'VE GOT YOUR PROOF!

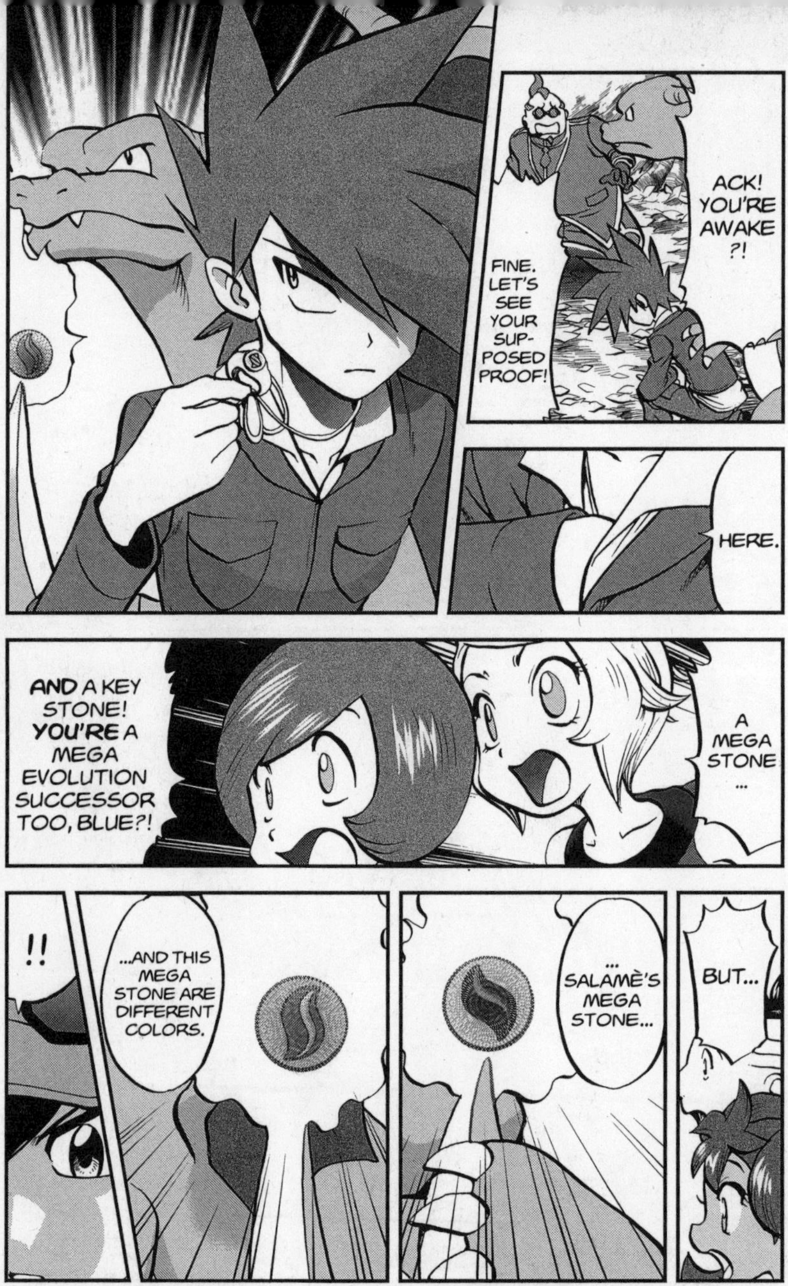
ACK! YOU'RE AWAKE ?!
FINE. LET'S SEE YOUR SUP-POSED PROOF!
HERE.
A MEGA STONE ...
AND A KEY STONE! **YOU'RE** A MEGA EVOLUTION SUCCESSOR TOO, BLUE?!
BUT...
... SALAMÈ'S MEGA STONE...
...AND THIS MEGA STONE ARE DIFFERENT COLORS.
!!

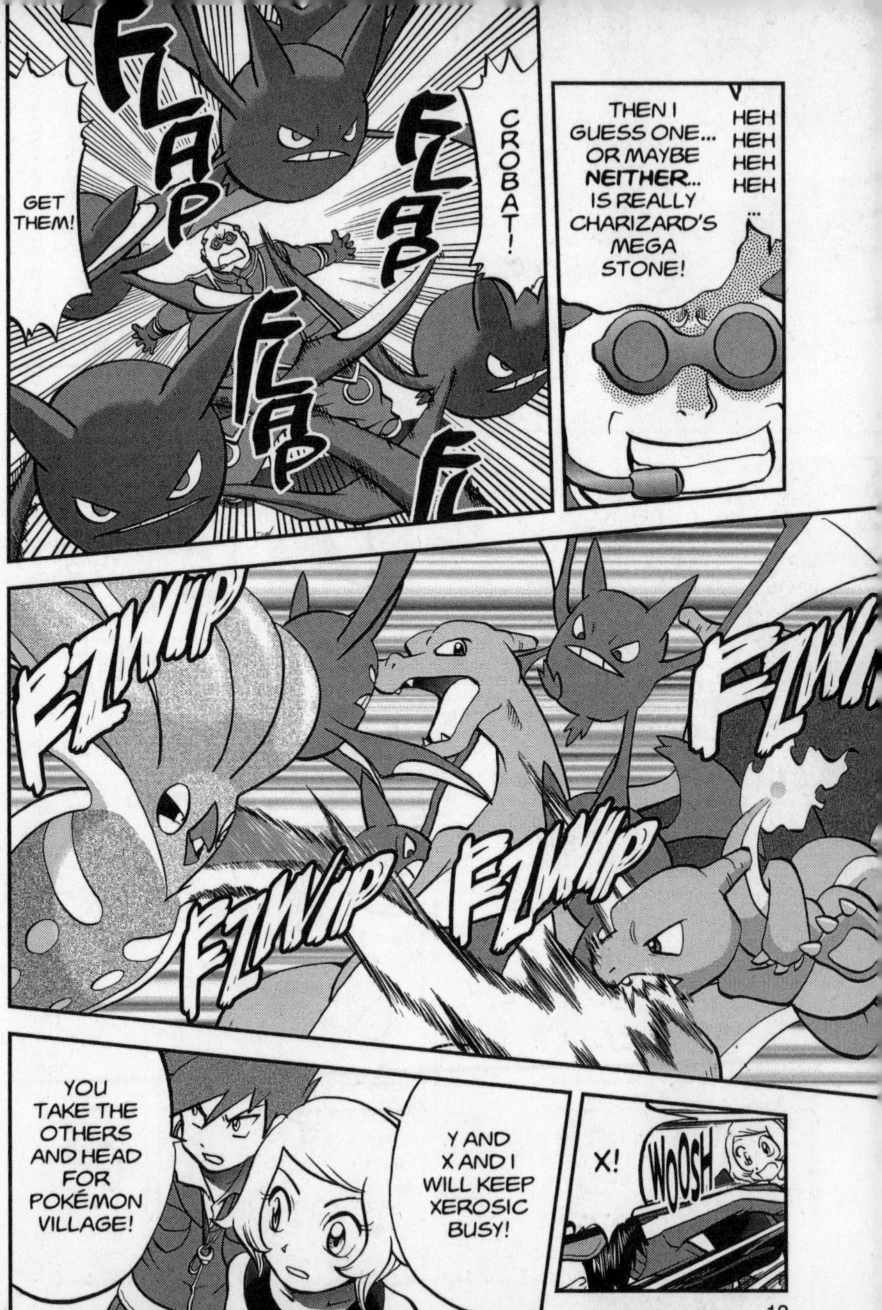
THEN I GUESS ONE... OR MAYBE NEITHER... IS REALLY CHARIZARD'S MEGA STONE!
HEH HEH HEH HEH ...
CROBAT!
FLAP FLAP FLAP FL
FLAP
GET THEM!
FZWIP
FZWIP
FZWIP
FZWIP
X!
WOOSH
Y AND X AND I WILL KEEP XEROSIC BUSY!
YOU TAKE THE OTHERS AND HEAD FOR POKÉMON VILLAGE!

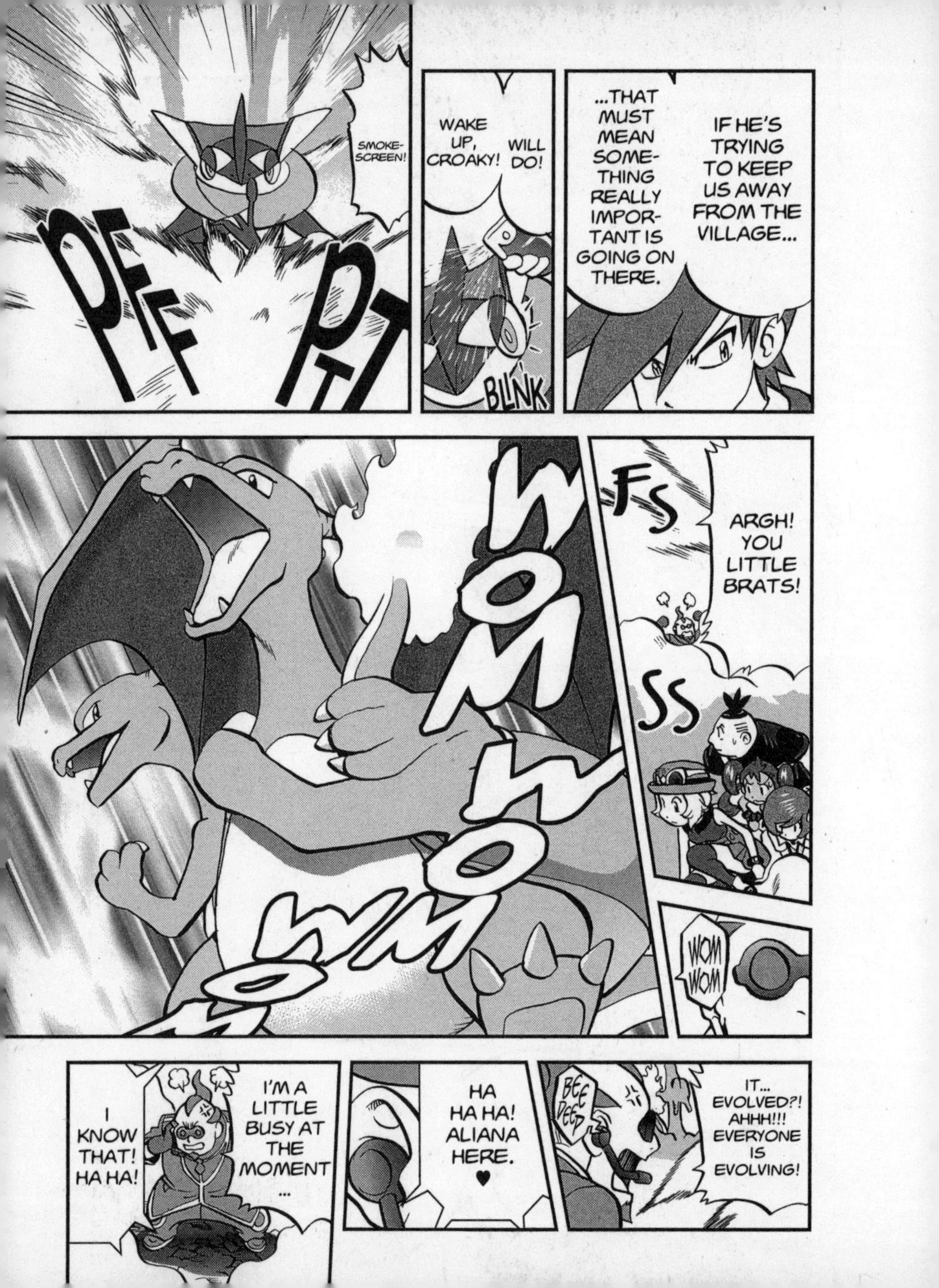
IF HE'S TRYING TO KEEP US AWAY FROM THE VILLAGE...
...THAT MUST MEAN SOMETHING REALLY IMPORTANT IS GOING ON THERE.
WILL DO!
WAKE UP, CROAKY!
BLINK
SMOKESCREEN!
PFFF
PTT
ARGH! YOU LITTLE BRATS!
FS
SS
WOM WOM
WOMWOMWOM
IT... EVOLVED?! AHHH!!! EVERYONE IS EVOLVING!
BEE DEEP
HA HA HA! ALIANA HERE. ♥
I'M A LITTLE BUSY AT THE MOMENT...
I KNOW THAT! HA HA!

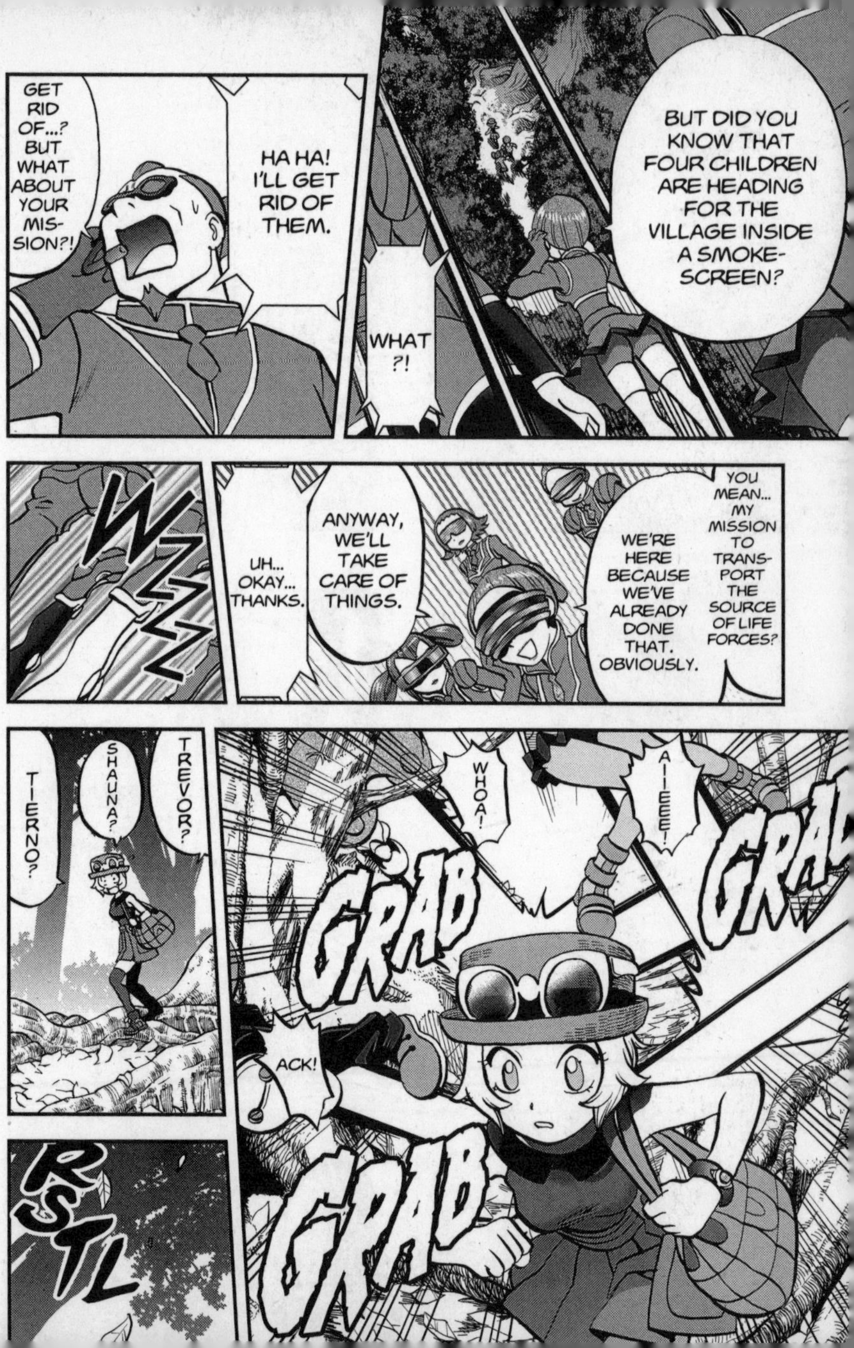
BUT DID YOU KNOW THAT FOUR CHILDREN ARE HEADING FOR THE VILLAGE INSIDE A SMOKE-SCREEN?
WHAT?!
HA HA! I'LL GET RID OF THEM.
GET RID OF...? BUT WHAT ABOUT YOUR MIS-SION?!
YOU MEAN... MY MISSION TO TRANS-PORT THE SOURCE OF LIFE FORCES?
WE'RE HERE BECAUSE WE'VE ALREADY DONE THAT. OBVIOUSLY.
ANYWAY, WE'LL TAKE CARE OF THINGS.
UH... OKAY... THANKS.
WZZZ
AIIEEE!
WHOA!
CRAB
CRAB
ACK!
CRAB
TREVOR?
SHAUNA?
TIERNO?
RSTL

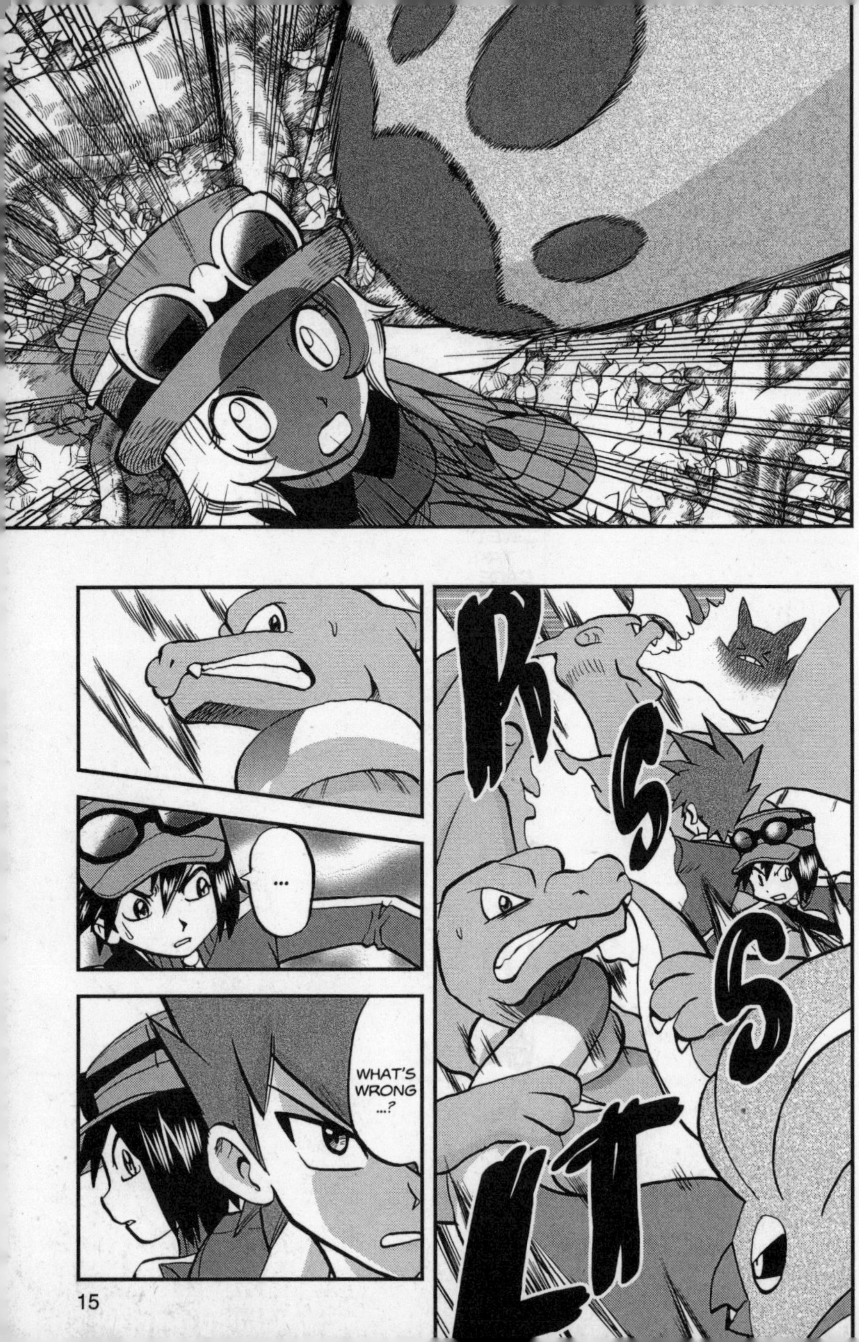
RSSLT
...
WHAT'S WRONG ...?

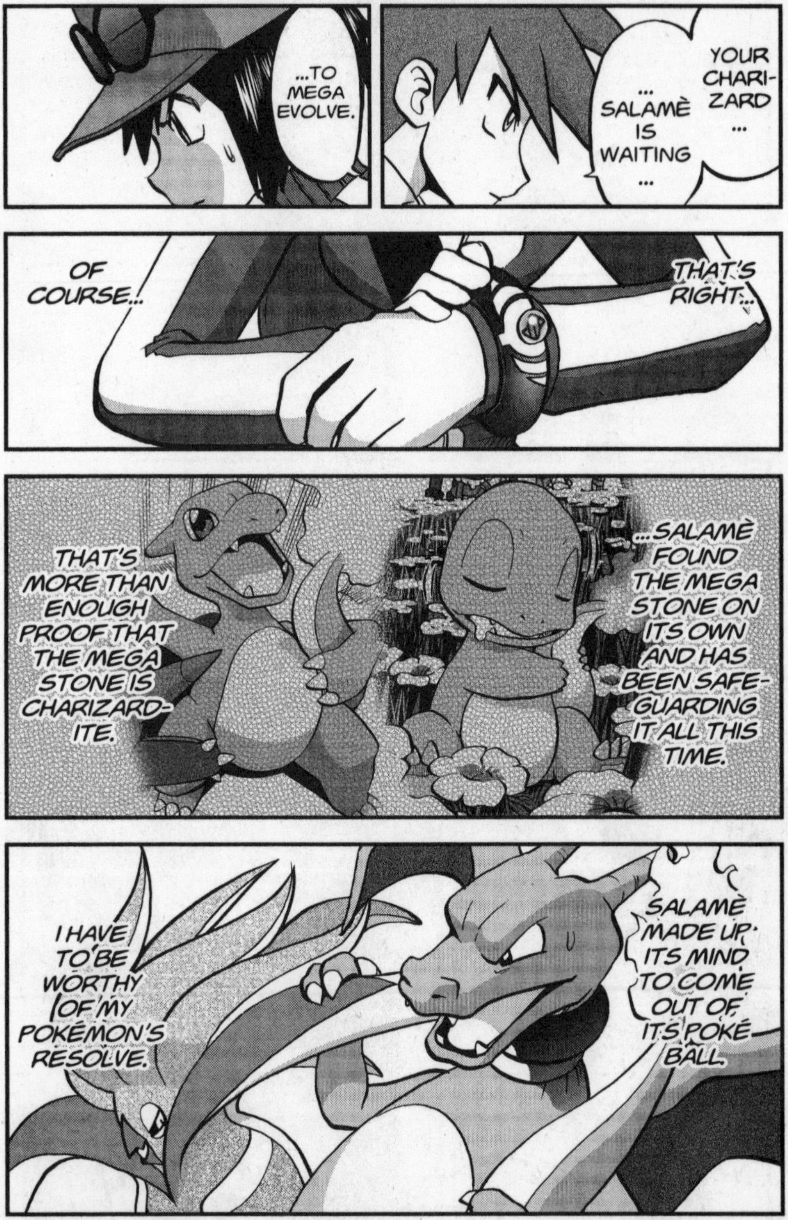
YOUR CHARI-ZARD ...
... SALAMÈ IS WAITING ...
...TO MEGA EVOLVE.
THAT'S RIGHT...
OF COURSE...
...SALAMÈ FOUND THE MEGA STONE ON ITS OWN AND HAS BEEN SAFE-GUARDING IT ALL THIS TIME.
THAT'S MORE THAN ENOUGH PROOF THAT THE MEGA STONE IS CHARIZARD-ITE.
SALAMÈ MADE UP ITS MIND TO COME OUT OF ITS POKÉ BALL.
I HAVE TO BE WORTHY OF MY POKÉMON'S RESOLVE.

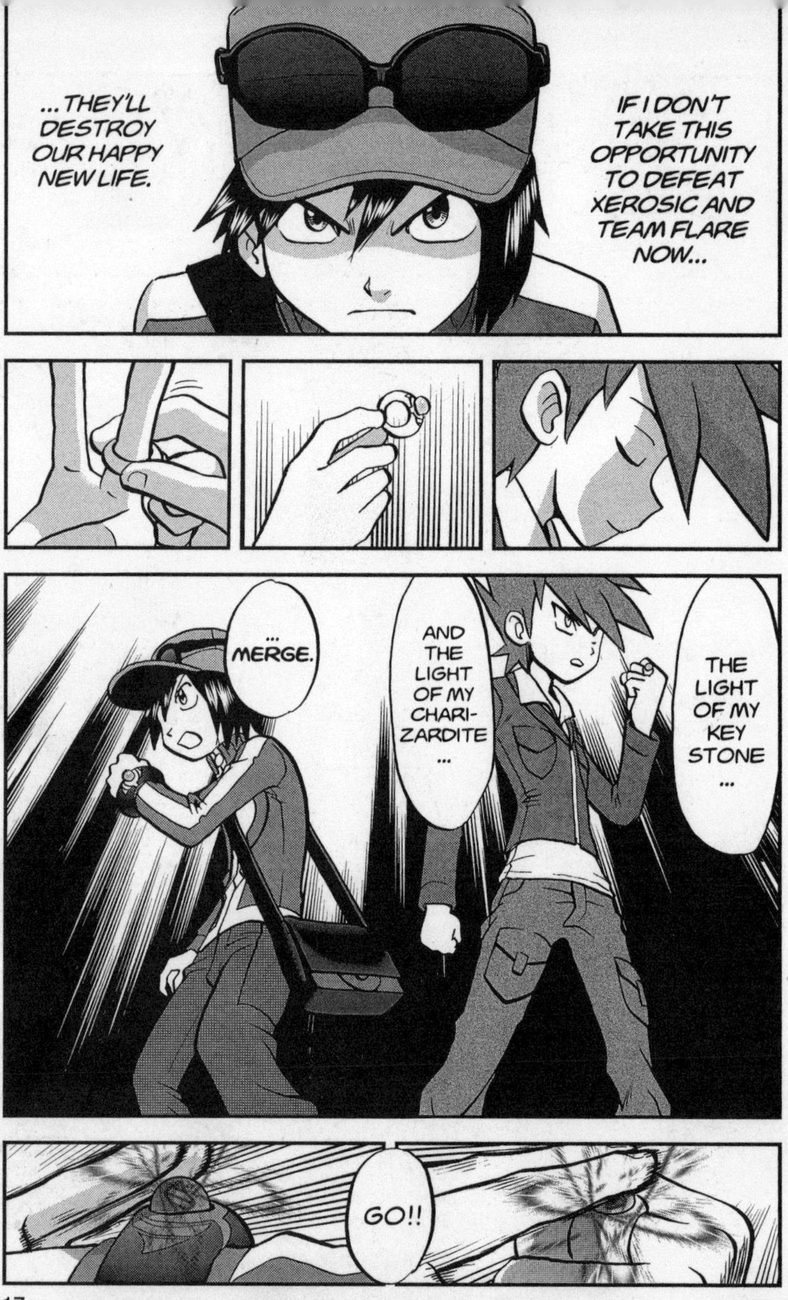
IF I DON'T TAKE THIS OPPORTUNITY TO DEFEAT XEROSIC AND TEAM FLARE NOW...
...THEY'LL DESTROY OUR HAPPY NEW LIFE.
THE LIGHT OF MY KEY STONE ...
AND THE LIGHT OF MY CHARI-ZARDITE ...
... MERGE.
GO!!

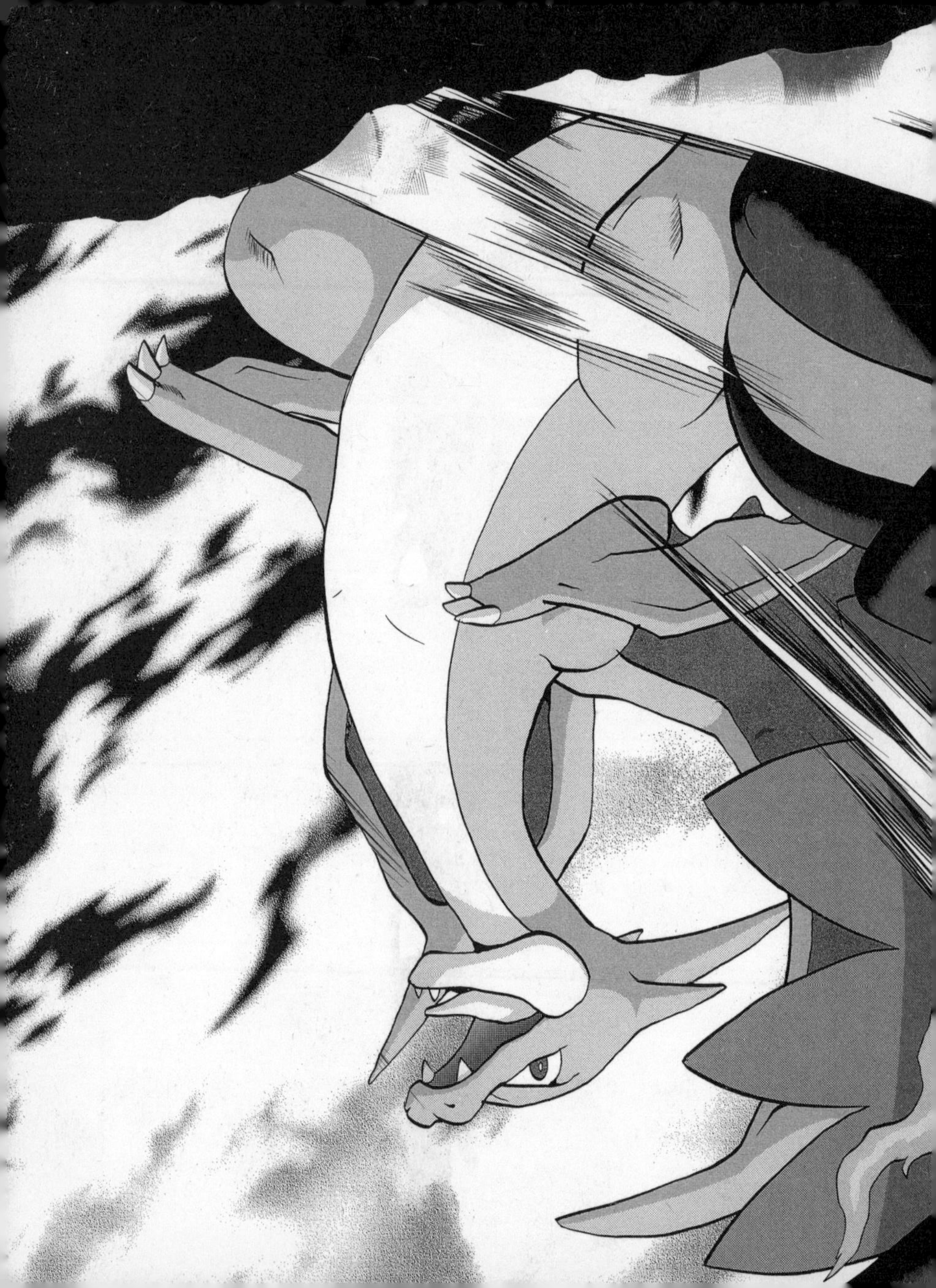

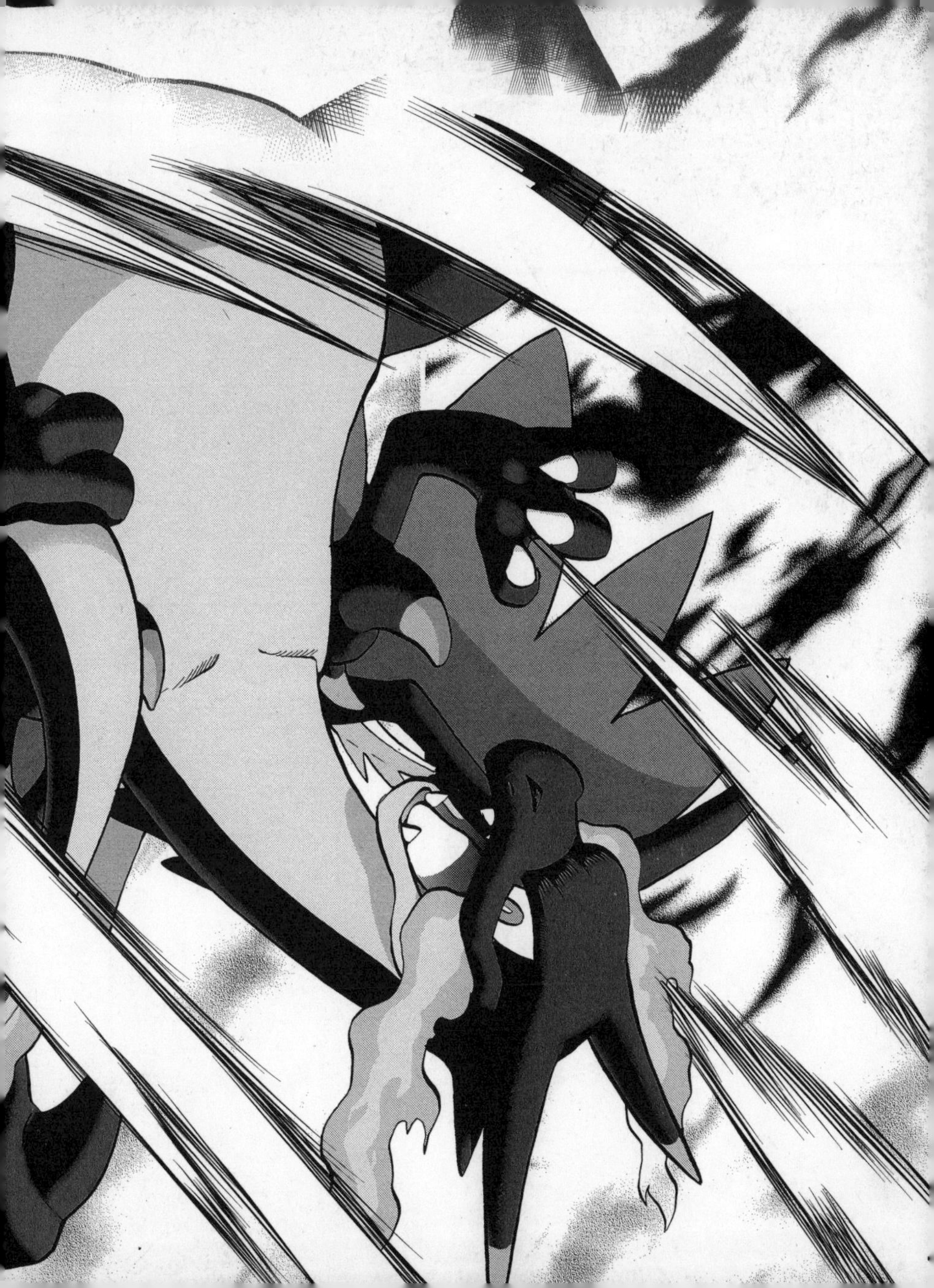

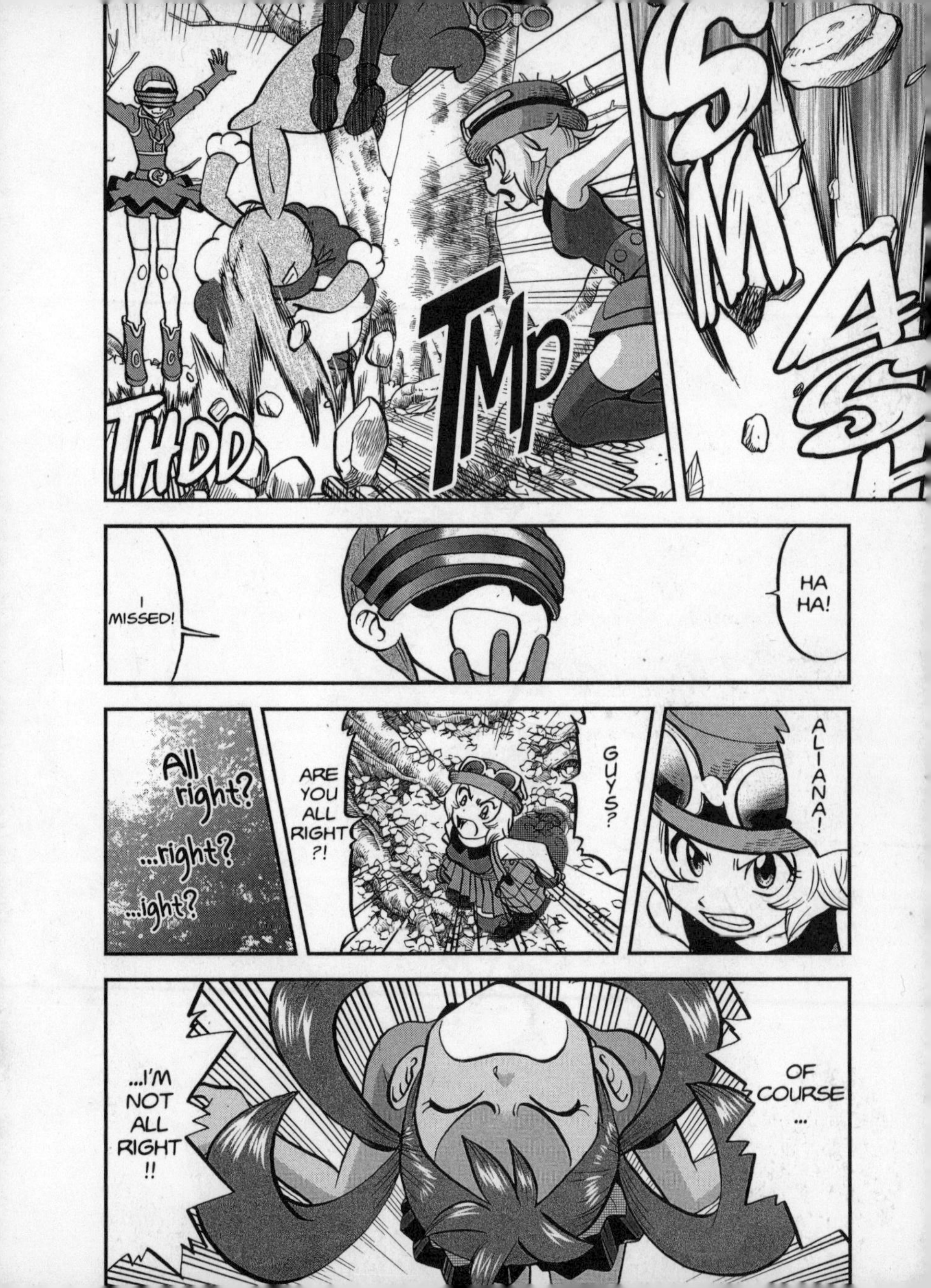
SMAS
TMP
THUD
HA HA!
I MISSED!
ALIANA!
GUYS?
ARE YOU ALL RIGHT ?!
All right?
...right?
...ight?
OF COURSE ...
...I'M NOT ALL RIGHT !!

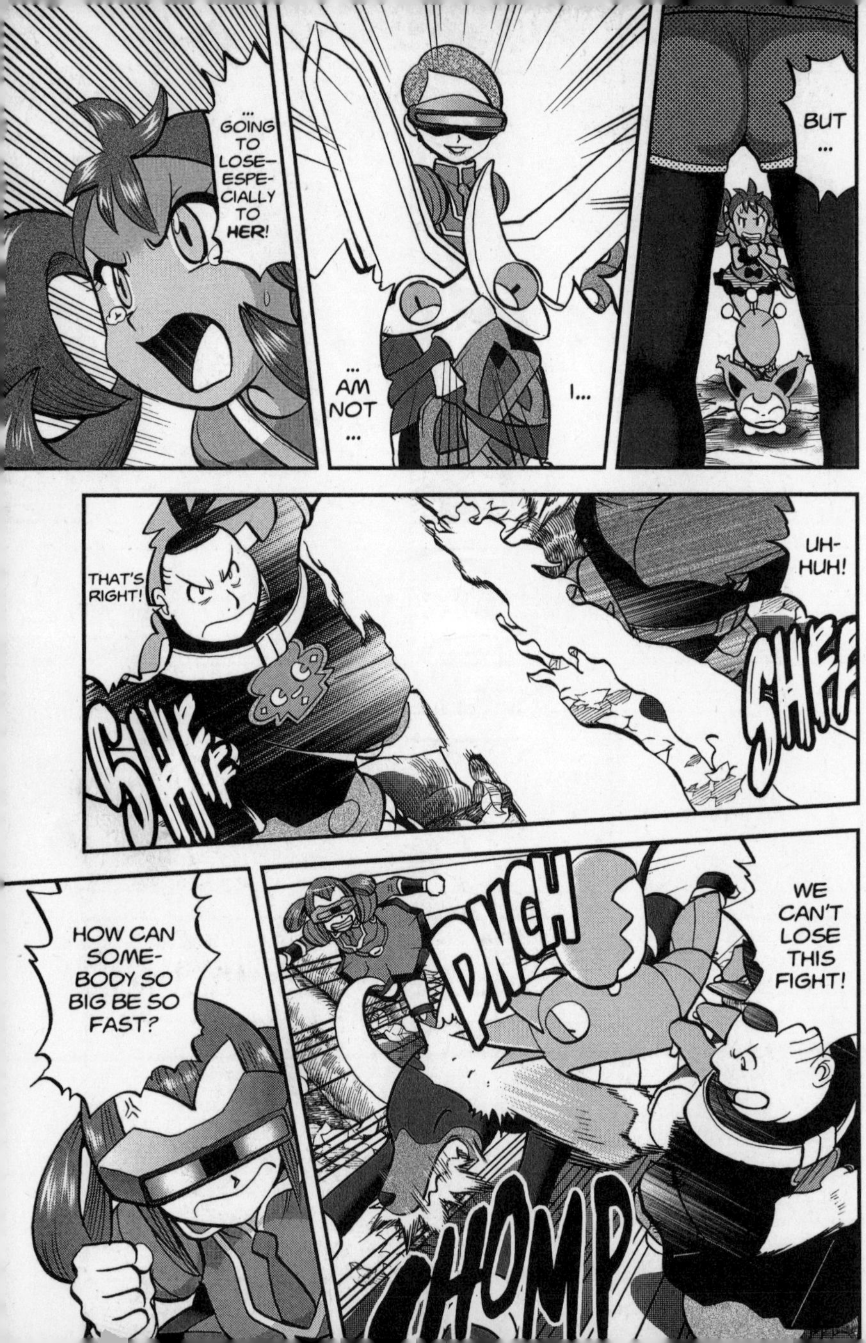
BUT ...
I...
...AM NOT ...
...GOING TO LOSE—ESPECIALLY TO HER!
UH-HUH!
SHFF
THAT'S RIGHT!
SHFF
WE CAN'T LOSE THIS FIGHT!
PNCH
CHOMP
HOW CAN SOMEBODY SO BIG BE SO FAST?

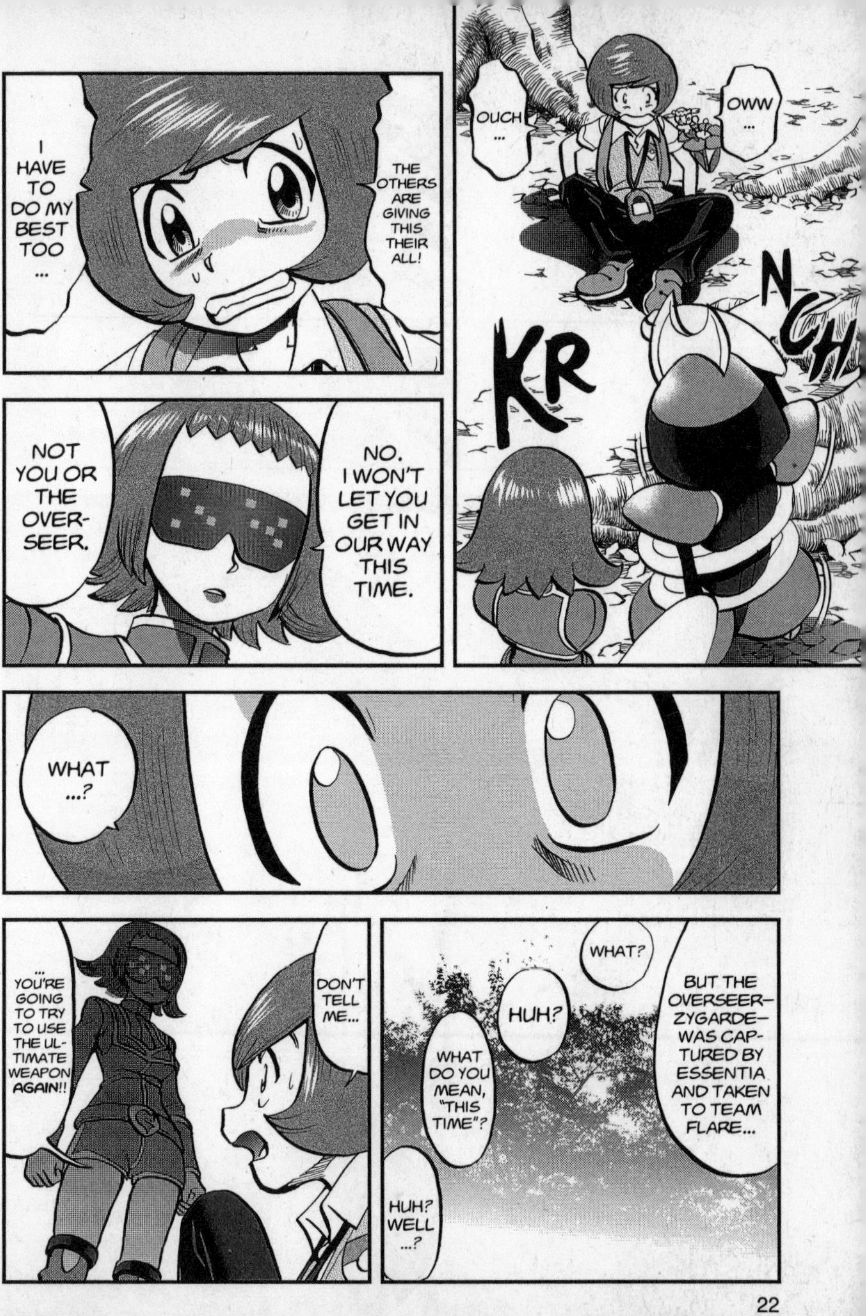
OWW ...
OUCH ...
KR NCH
THE OTHERS ARE GIVING THIS THEIR ALL!
I HAVE TO DO MY BEST TOO ...
NO. I WON'T LET YOU GET IN OUR WAY THIS TIME.
NOT YOU OR THE OVER-SEER.
WHAT ...?
BUT THE OVERSEER-ZYGARDE-WAS CAP-TURED BY ESSENTIA AND TAKEN TO TEAM FLARE...
WHAT?
HUH?
WHAT DO YOU MEAN, "THIS TIME"?
HUH? WELL ...?
DON'T TELL ME...
... YOU'RE GOING TO TRY TO USE THE UL-TIMATE WEAPON AGAIN!!

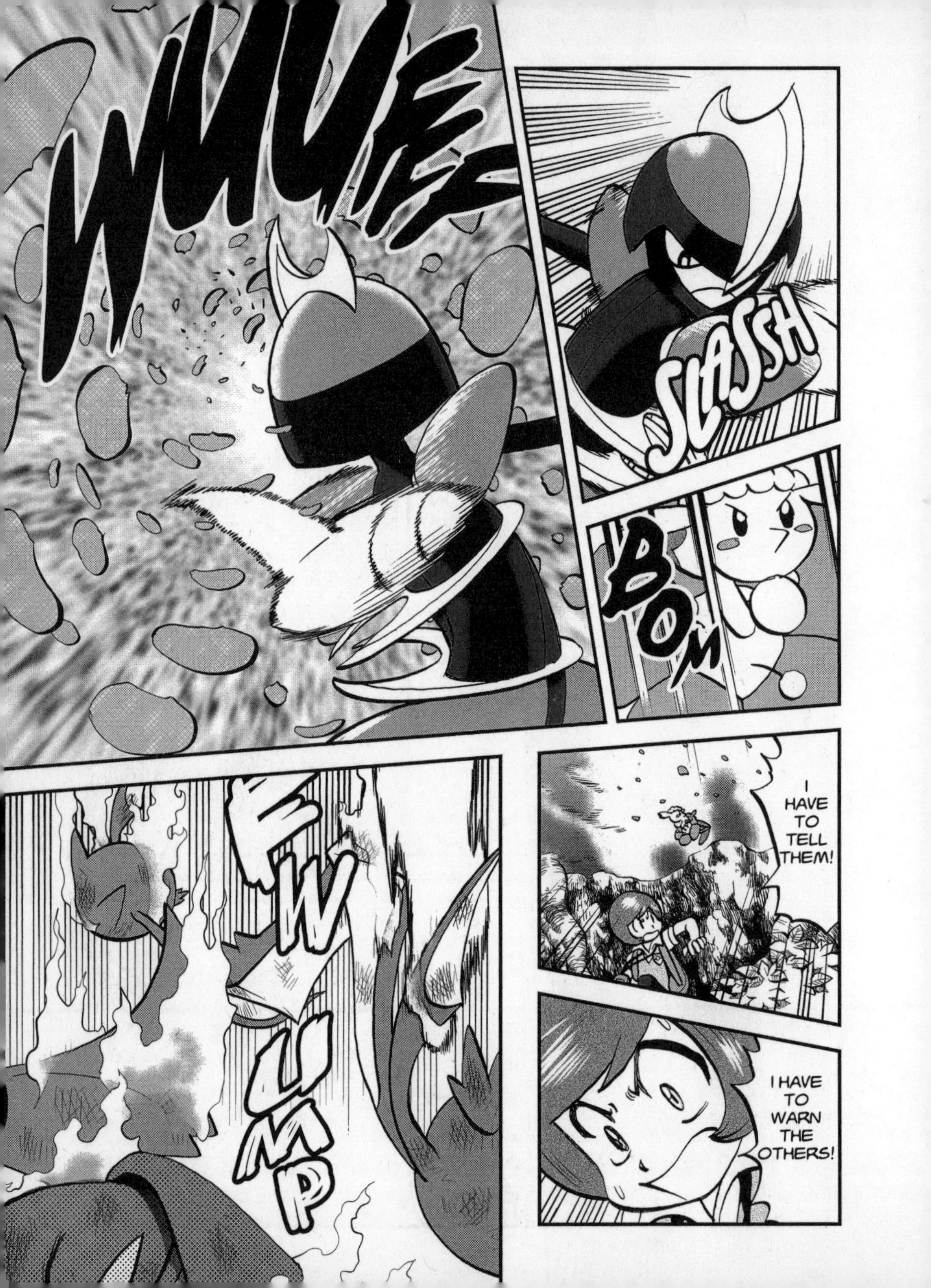
SLASSH
BOOM
WHUFF
I HAVE TO TELL THEM!
I HAVE TO WARN THE OTHERS!
FWUMP

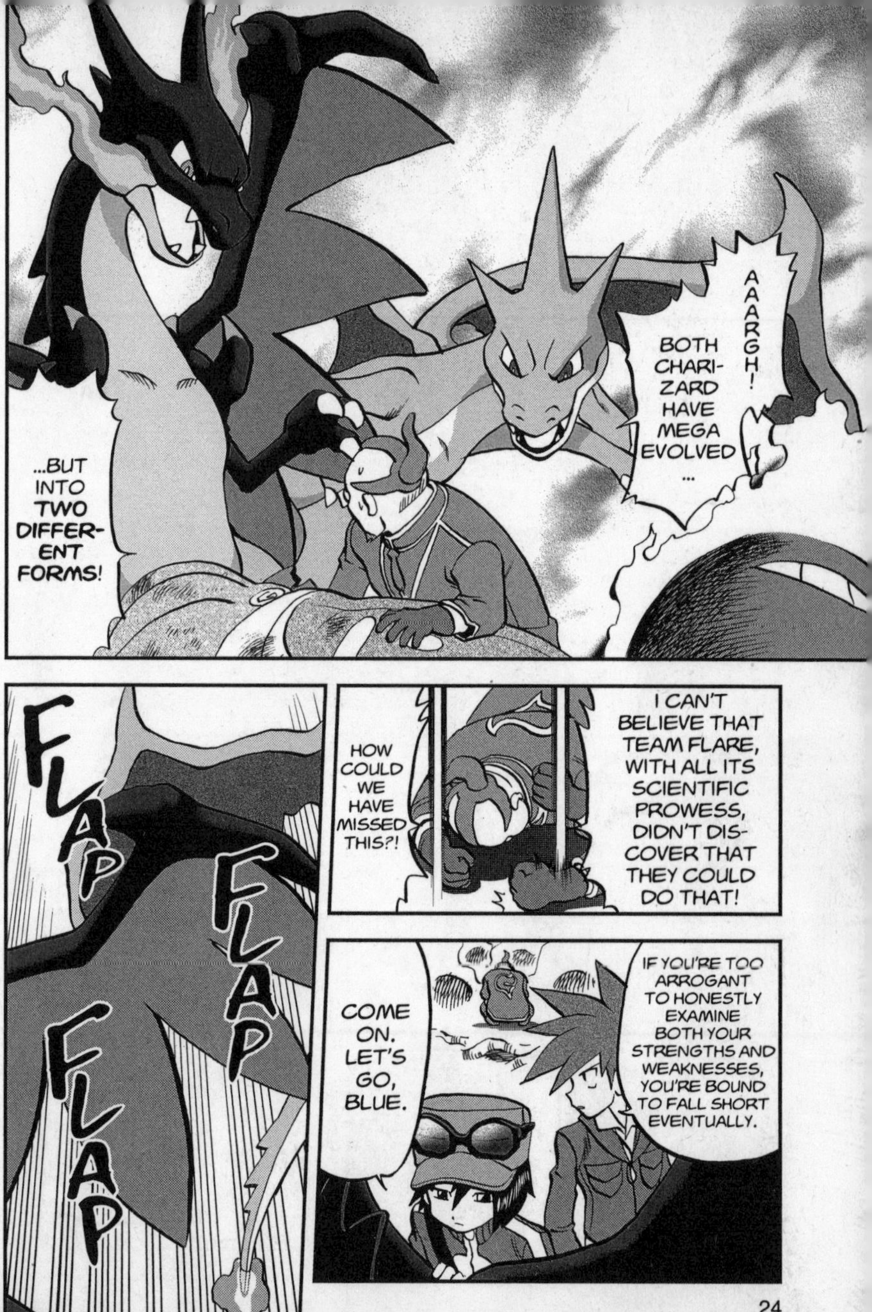
AAAARGH!
BOTH CHARIZARD HAVE MEGA EVOLVED...
...BUT INTO TWO DIFFERENT FORMS!
I CAN'T BELIEVE THAT TEAM FLARE, WITH ALL ITS SCIENTIFIC PROWESS, DIDN'T DISCOVER THAT THEY COULD DO THAT!
HOW COULD WE HAVE MISSED THIS?!
IF YOU'RE TOO ARROGANT TO HONESTLY EXAMINE BOTH YOUR STRENGTHS AND WEAKNESSES, YOU'RE BOUND TO FALL SHORT EVENTUALLY.
COME ON. LET'S GO, BLUE.
FLAP
FLAP
FLAP
FLAP

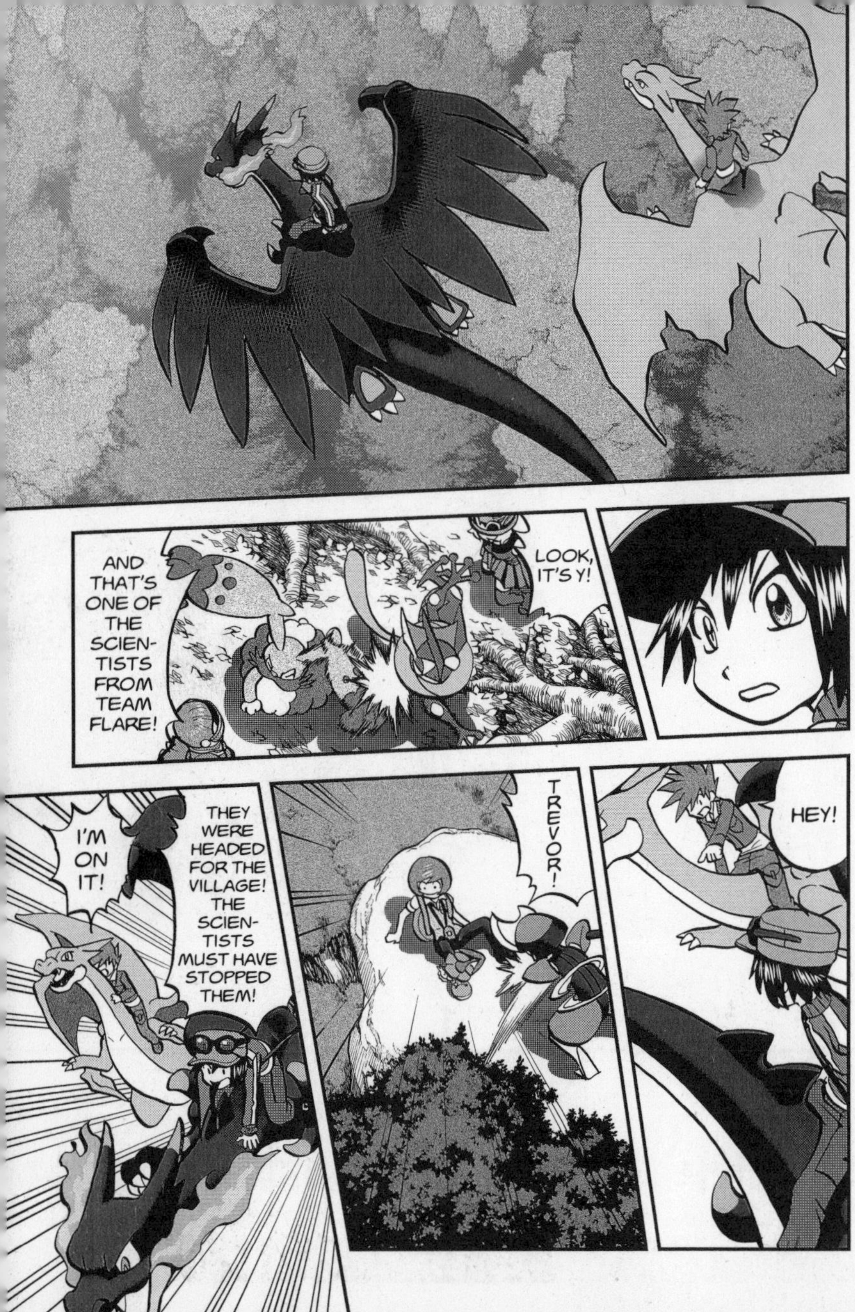
LOOK, IT'S Y!
AND THAT'S ONE OF THE SCIENTISTS FROM TEAM FLARE!
HEY!
TREVOR!
THEY WERE HEADED FOR THE VILLAGE! THE SCIENTISTS MUST HAVE STOPPED THEM!
I'M ON IT!

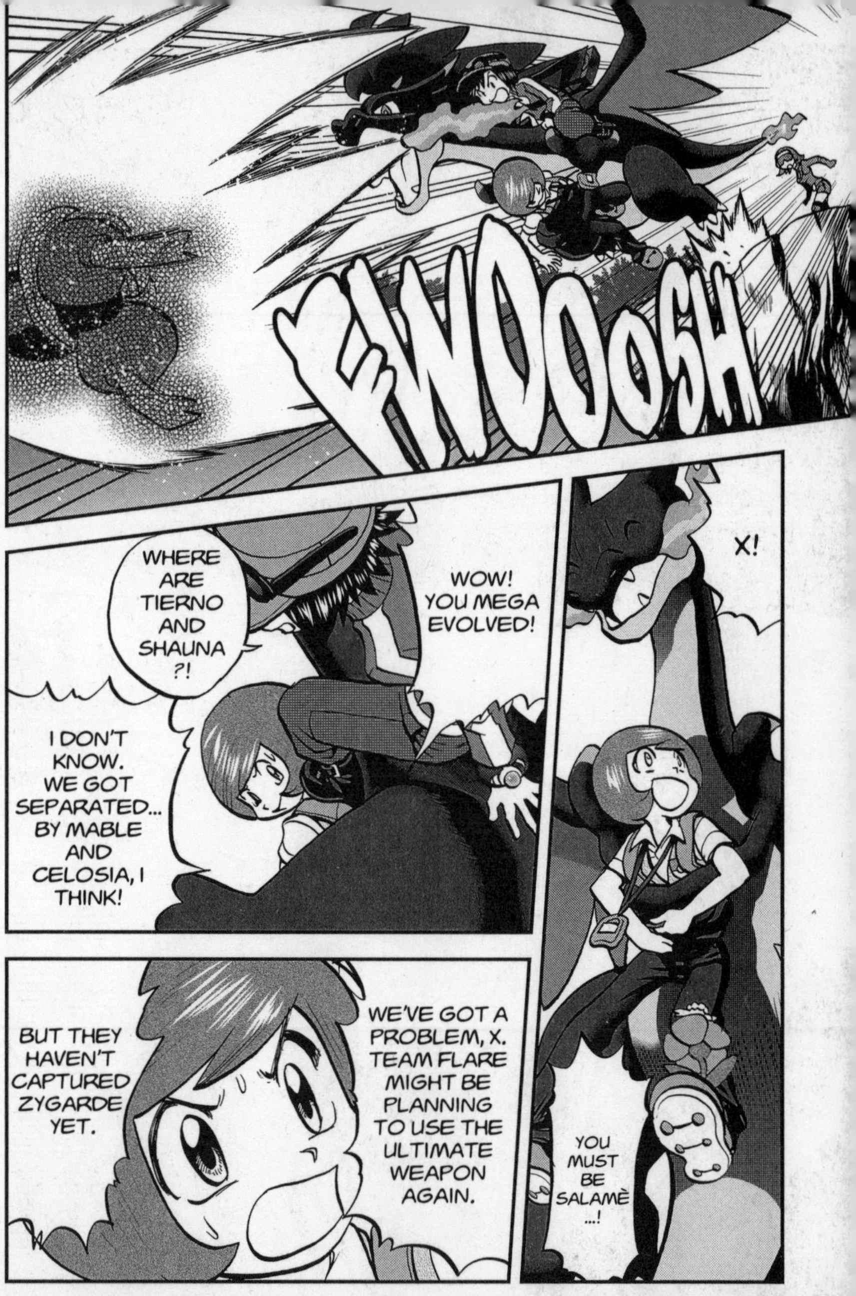
WHOOSH
X!
YOU MUST BE SALAMÈ ...!
WOW! YOU MEGA EVOLVED!
WHERE ARE TIERNO AND SHAUNA ?!
I DON'T KNOW. WE GOT SEPARATED... BY MABLE AND CELOSIA, I THINK!
WE'VE GOT A PROBLEM, X. TEAM FLARE MIGHT BE PLANNING TO USE THE ULTIMATE WEAPON AGAIN.
BUT THEY HAVEN'T CAPTURED ZYGARDE YET.

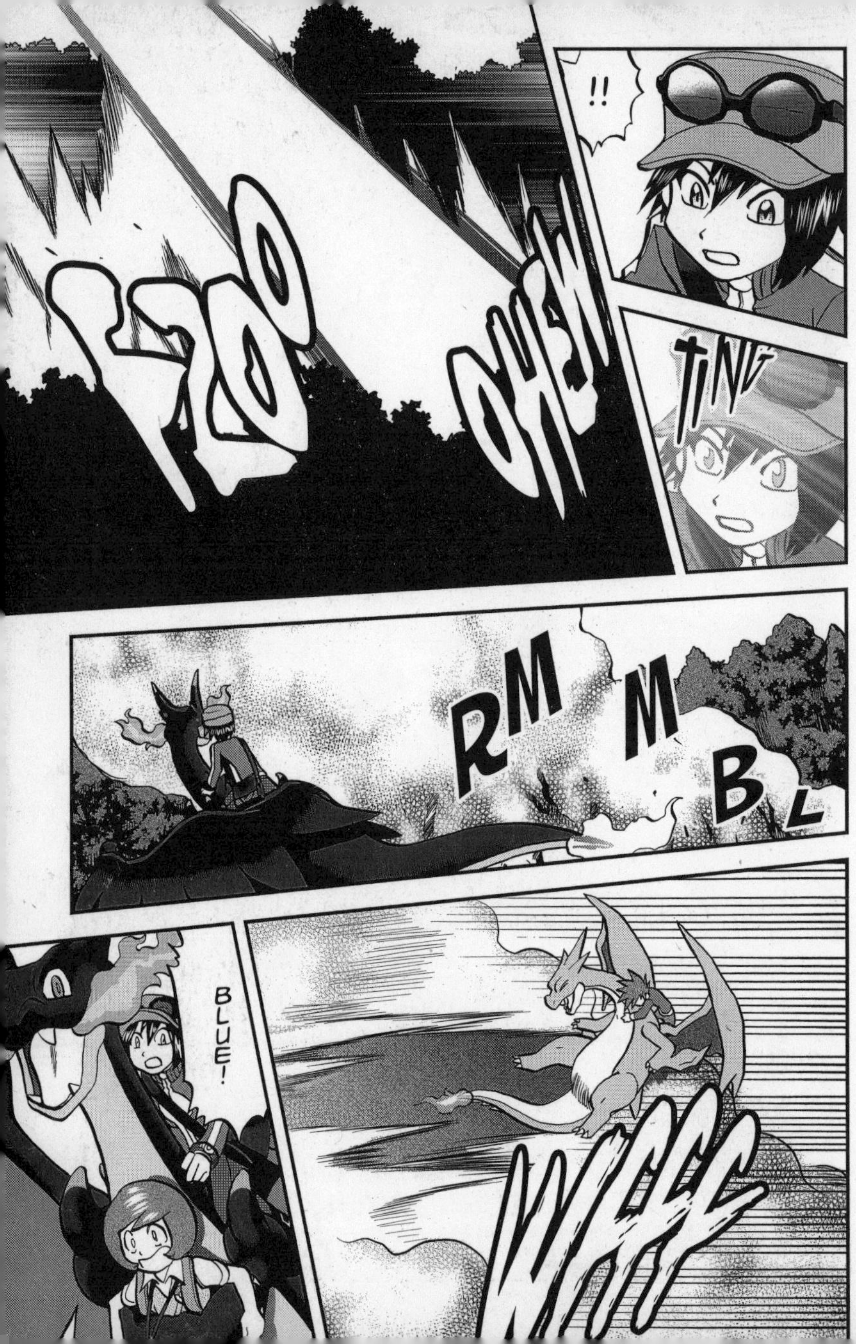
!!
RM
M
B
L
BLUE!

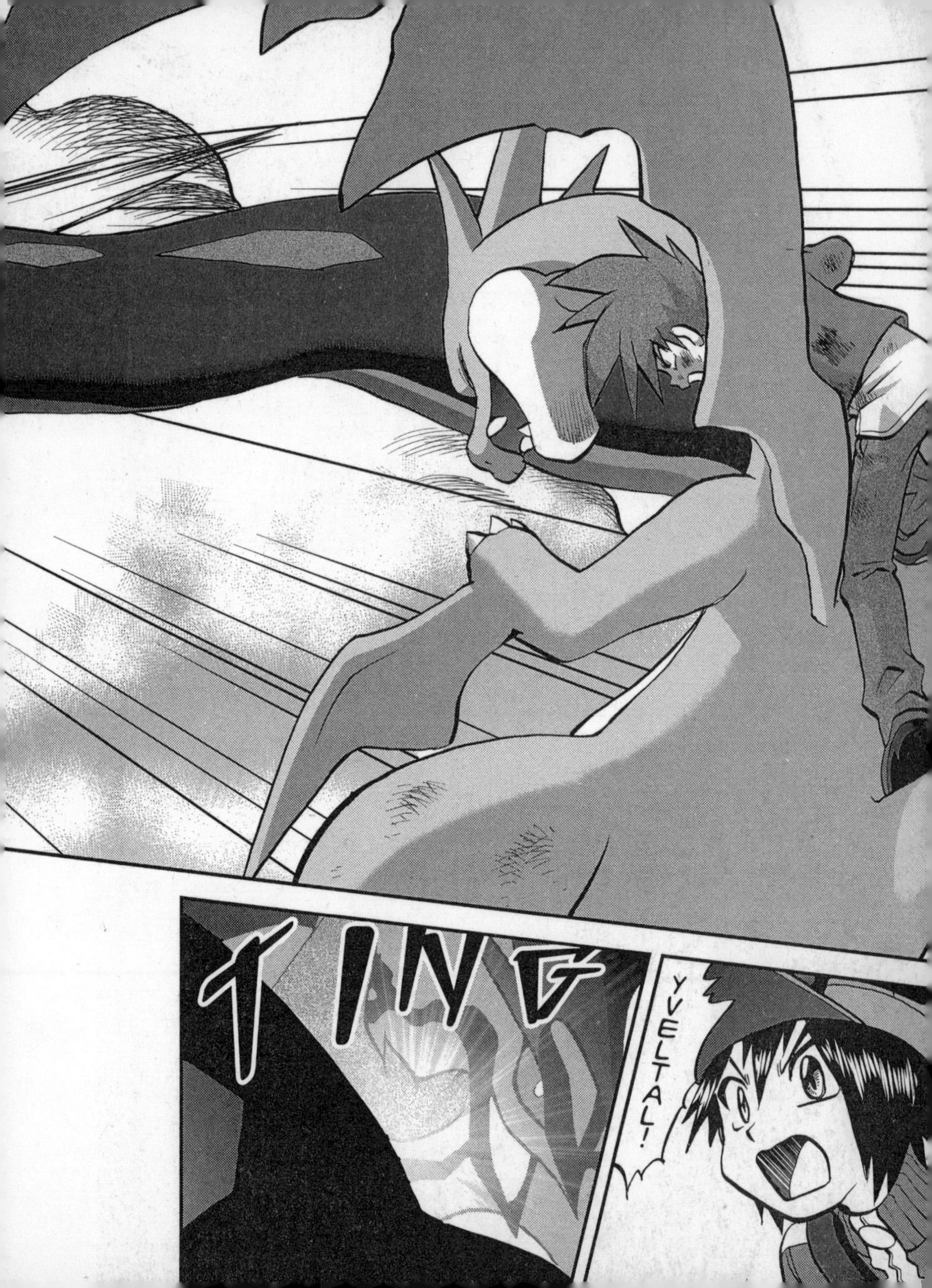
YVELTAL!
TING

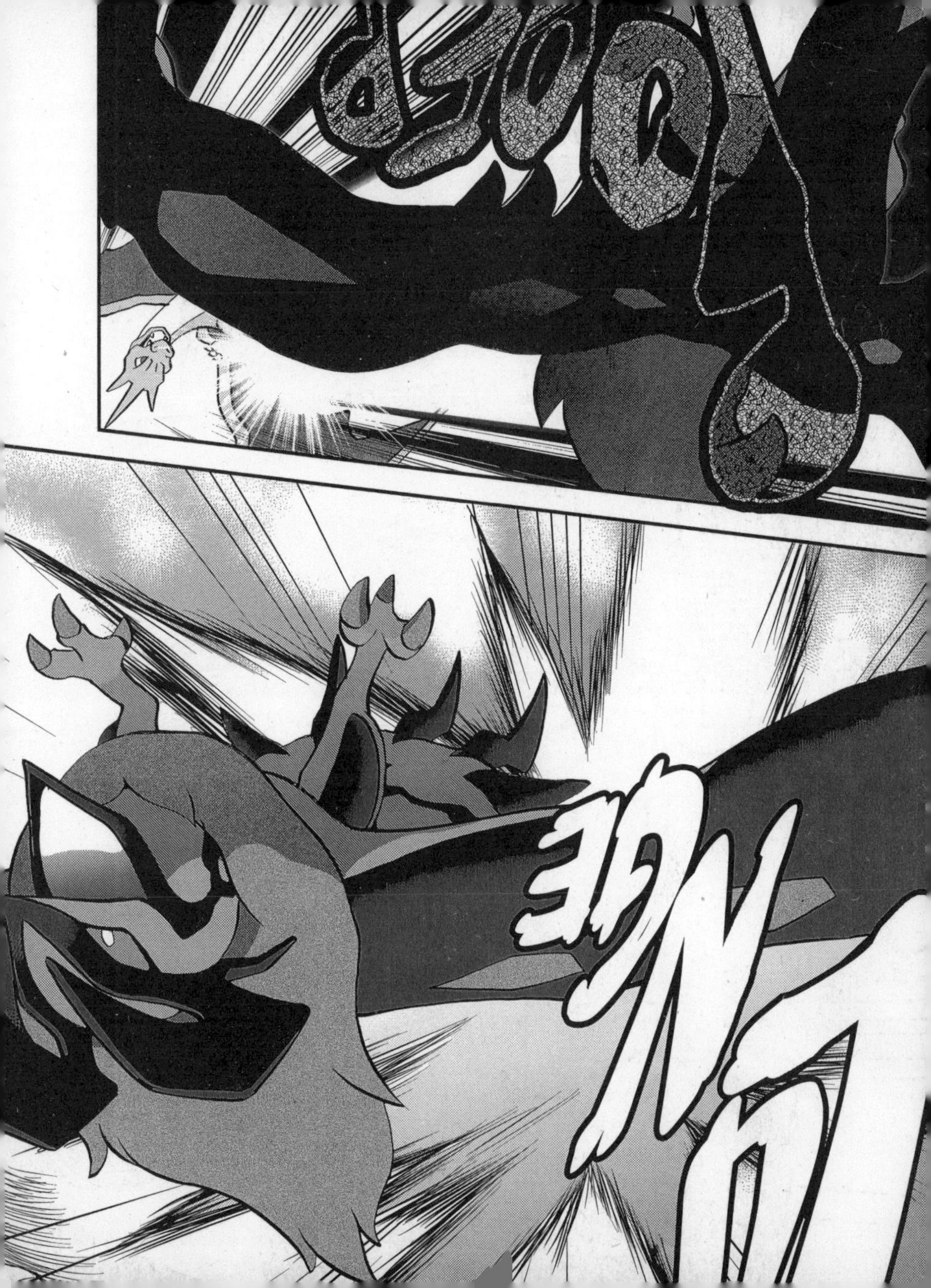

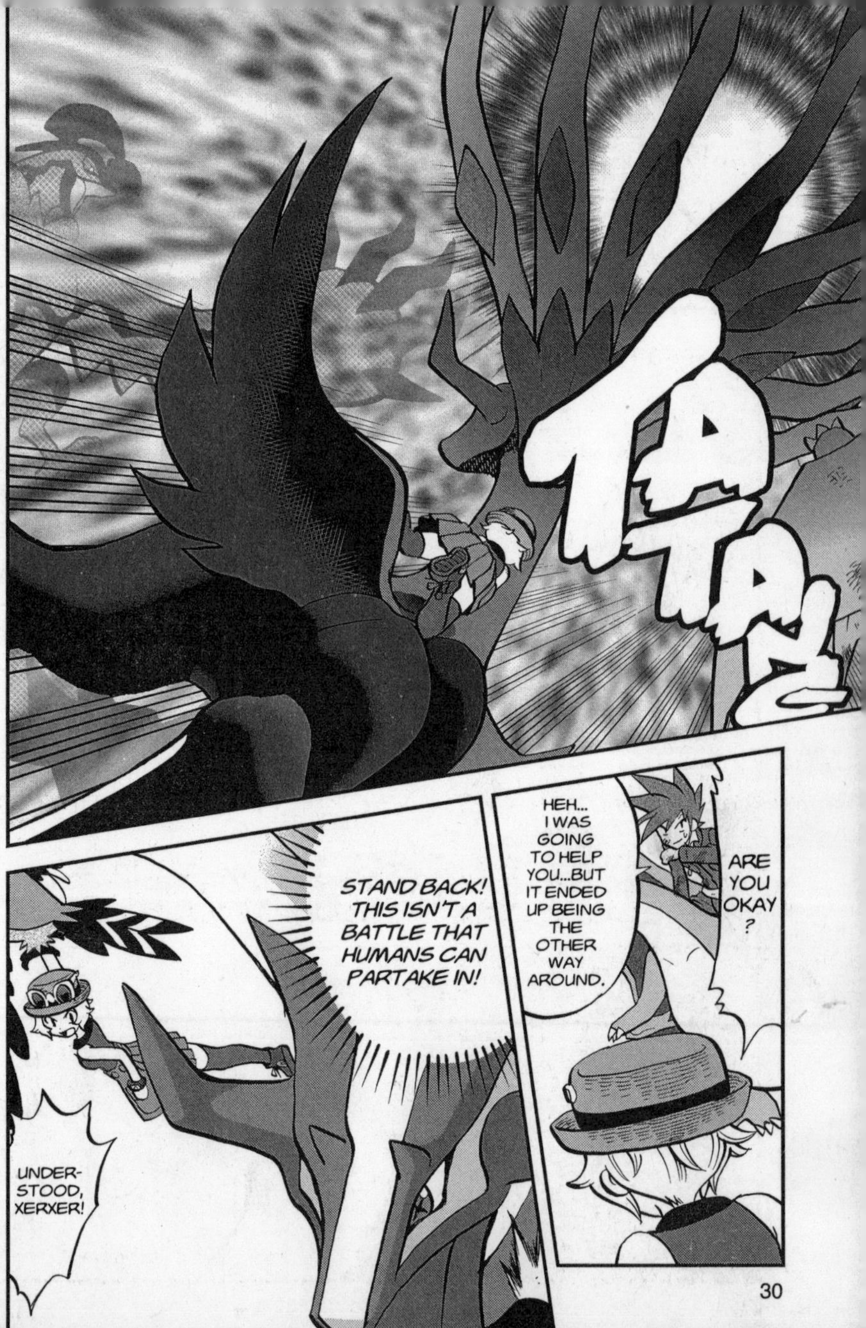
TA TA
ARE YOU OKAY ?
HEH... I WAS GOING TO HELP YOU...BUT IT ENDED UP BEING THE OTHER WAY AROUND.
STAND BACK! THIS ISN'T A BATTLE THAT HUMANS CAN PARTAKE IN!
UNDER-STOOD, XERXER!

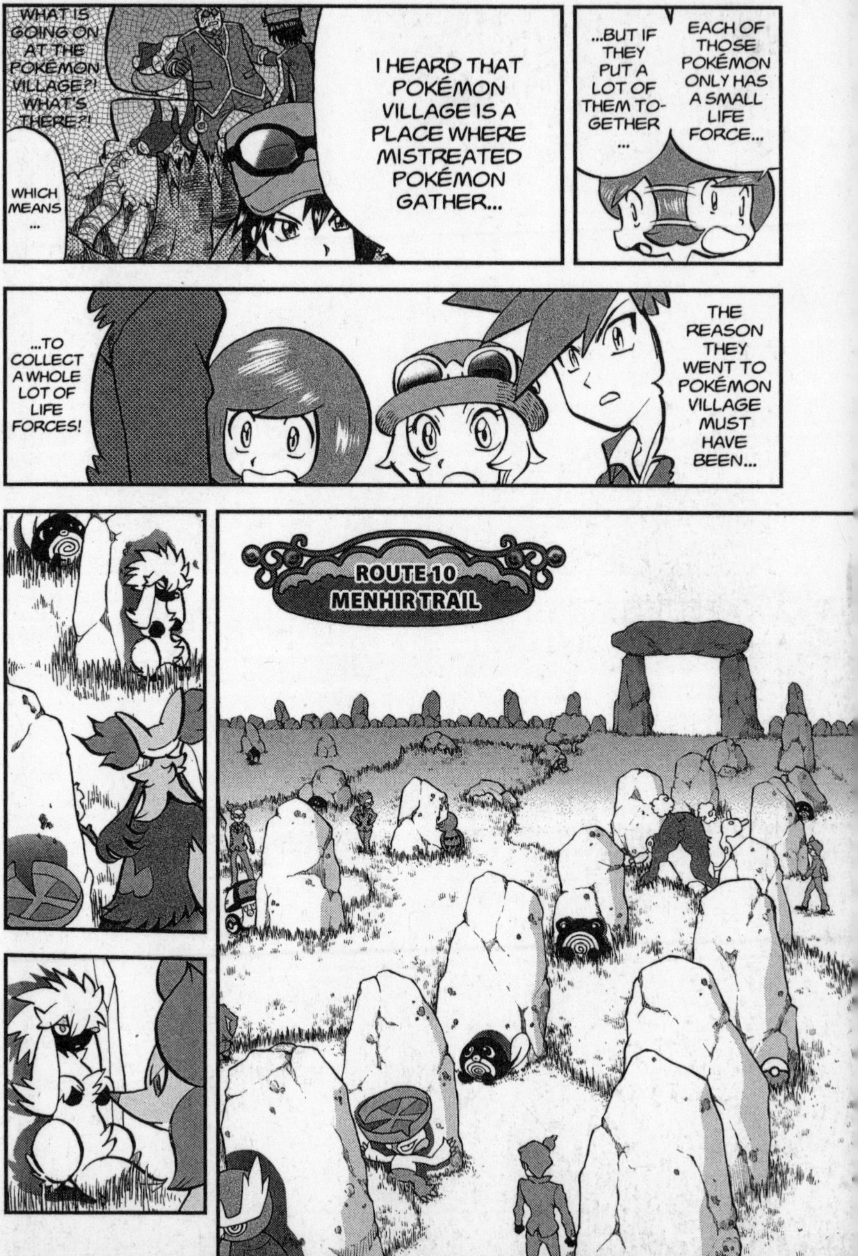
EACH OF THOSE POKÉMON ONLY HAS A SMALL LIFE FORCE...
...BUT IF THEY PUT A LOT OF THEM TO-GETHER ...
I HEARD THAT POKÉMON VILLAGE IS A PLACE WHERE MISTREATED POKÉMON GATHER...
WHAT IS GOING ON AT THE POKÉMON VILLAGE?! WHAT'S THERE?!
WHICH MEANS ...
THE REASON THEY WENT TO POKÉMON VILLAGE MUST HAVE BEEN...
...TO COLLECT A WHOLE LOT OF LIFE FORCES!
ROUTE 10
MENHIR TRAIL

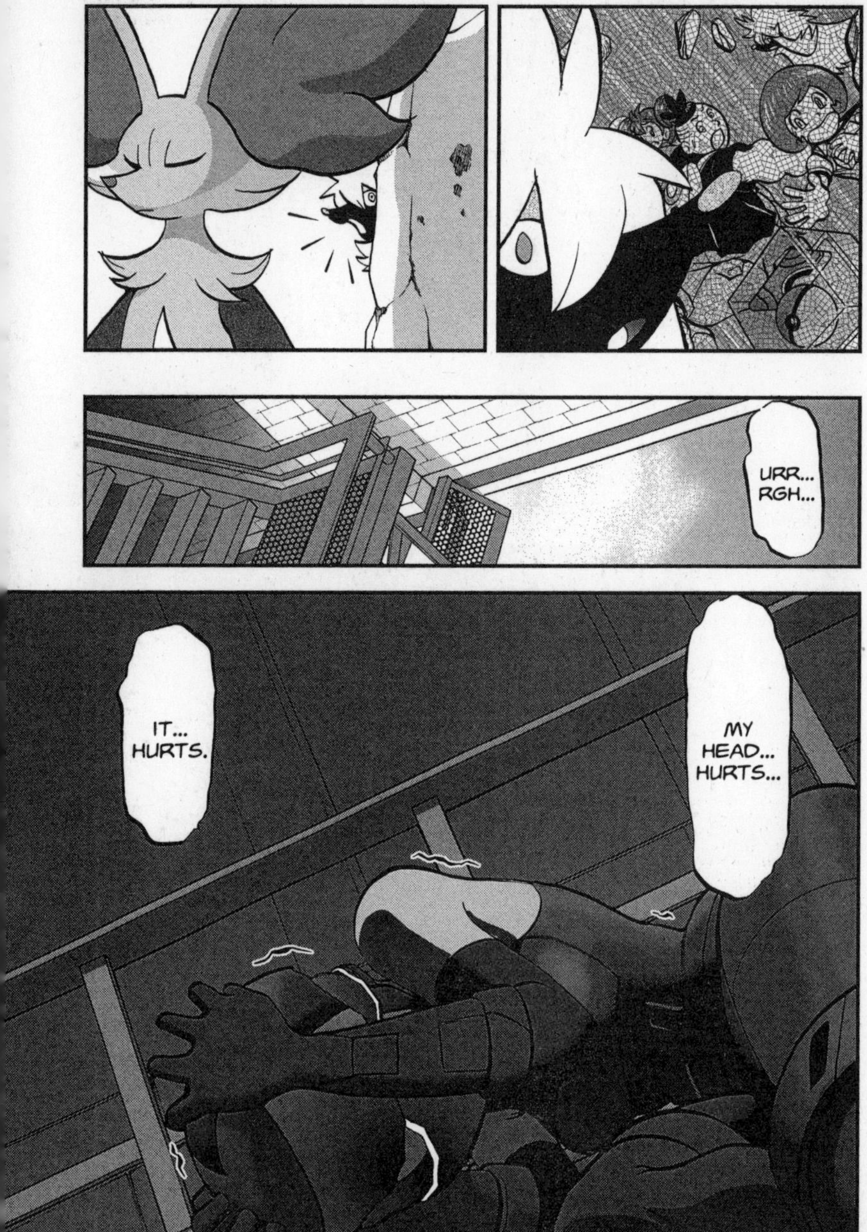
URR... RGH...
MY HEAD... HURTS...
IT... HURTS.

⊕ **Current Location**

Route 18
Vallée Étroite Way

This path is best known for its trolley, once used for the coal mine, and the curious Inverse Battle House.

Adventure 35 — Yveltal Steals

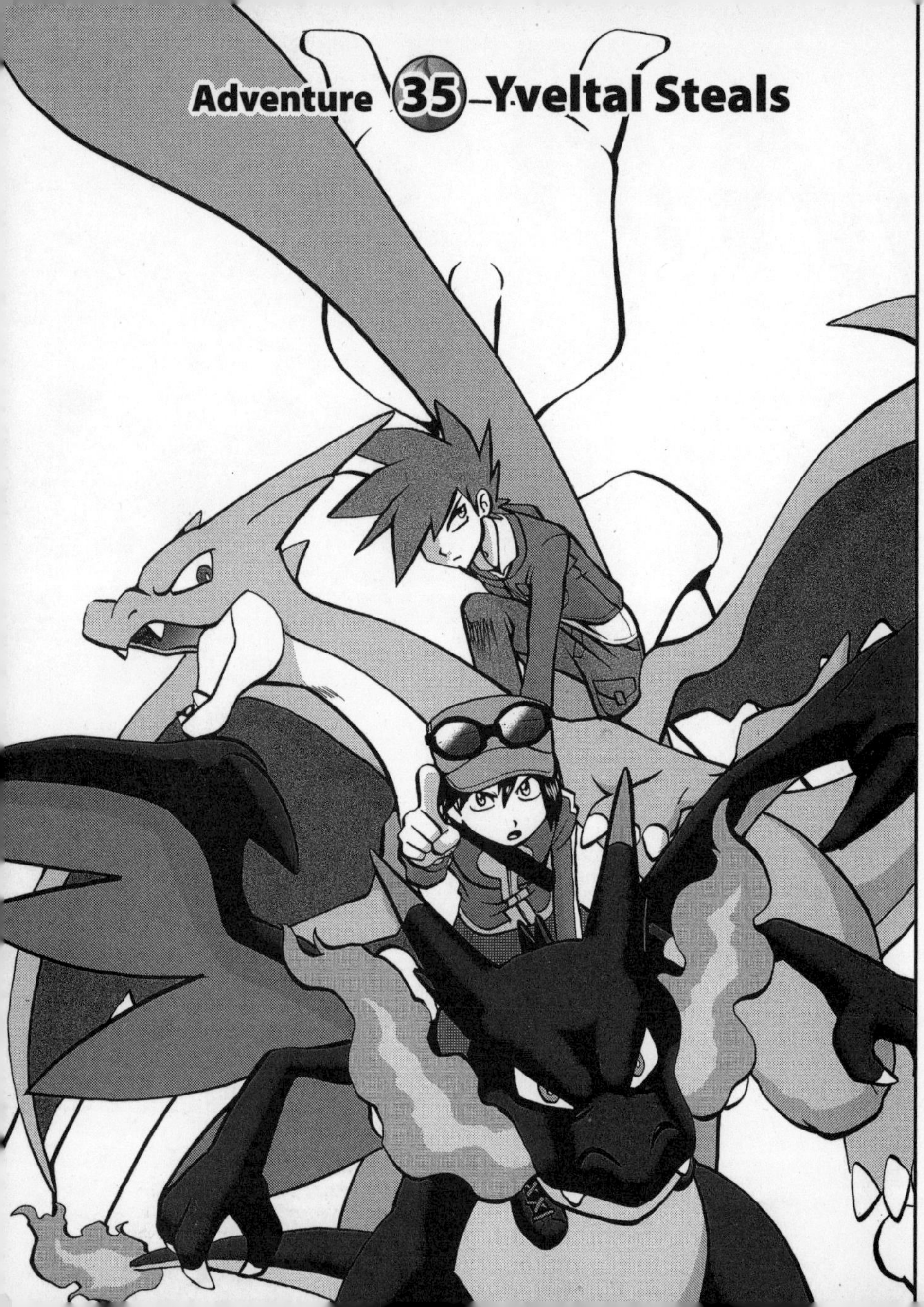

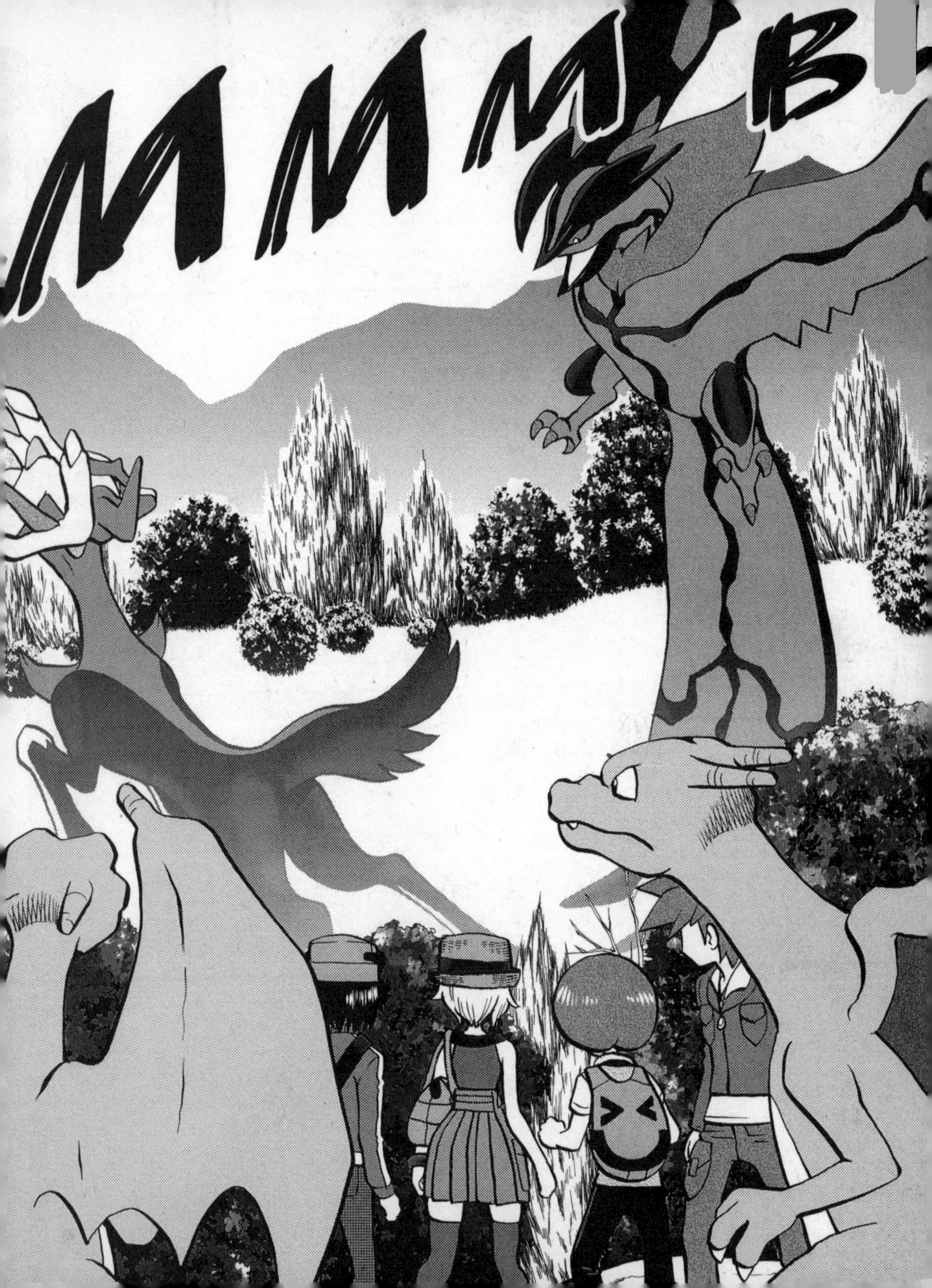

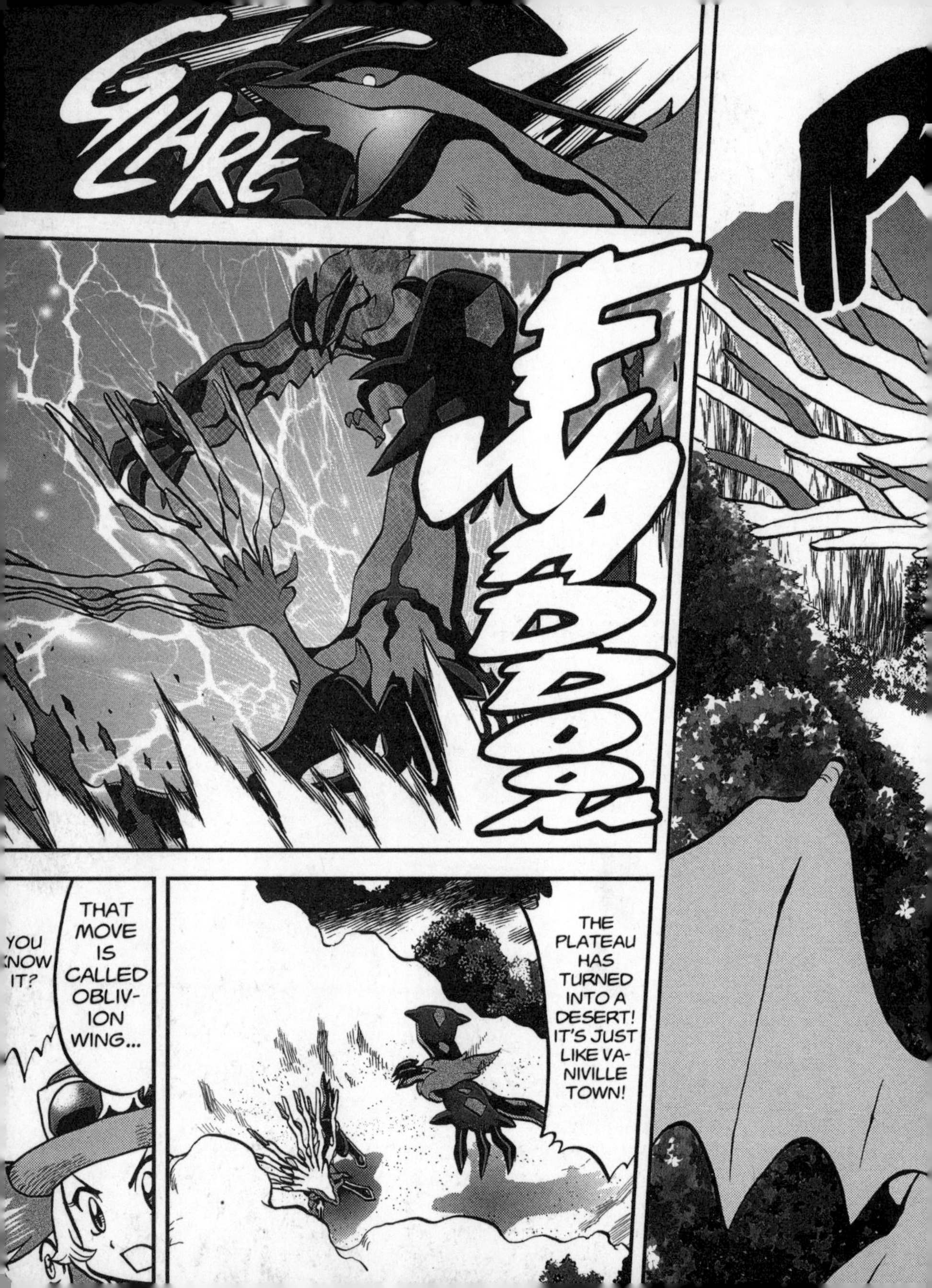
GLARE
FWADOOM
THE PLATEAU HAS TURNED INTO A DESERT! IT'S JUST LIKE VA-NIVILLE TOWN!
THAT MOVE IS CALLED OBLIV-ION WING...
YOU KNOW IT?

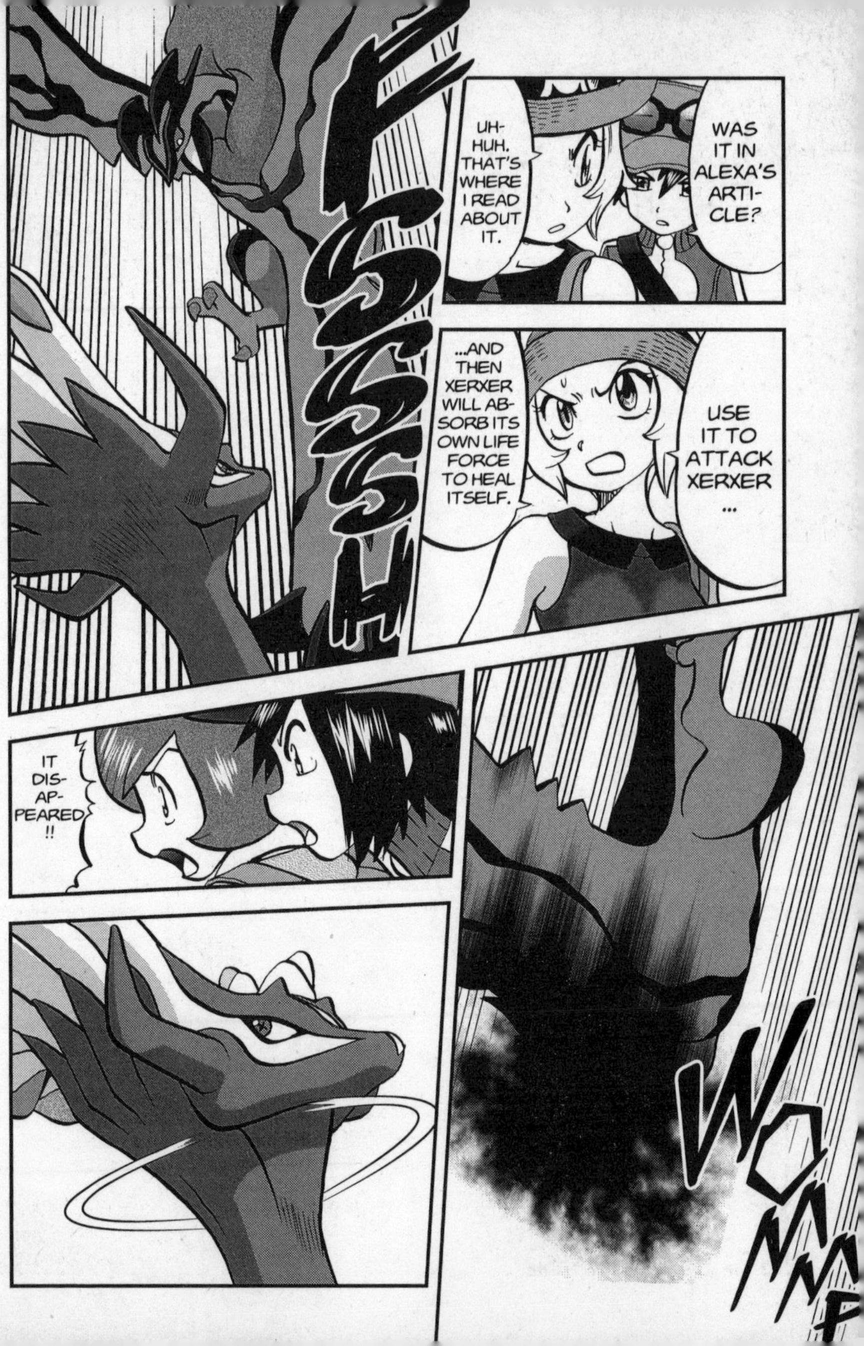
WAS IT IN ALEXA'S ARTI-CLE?
UH-HUH. THAT'S WHERE I READ ABOUT IT.
USE IT TO ATTACK XERXER ...
...AND THEN XERXER WILL AB-SORB ITS OWN LIFE FORCE TO HEAL ITSELF.
FSSSH
WOMMF
IT DIS-AP-PEARED !!

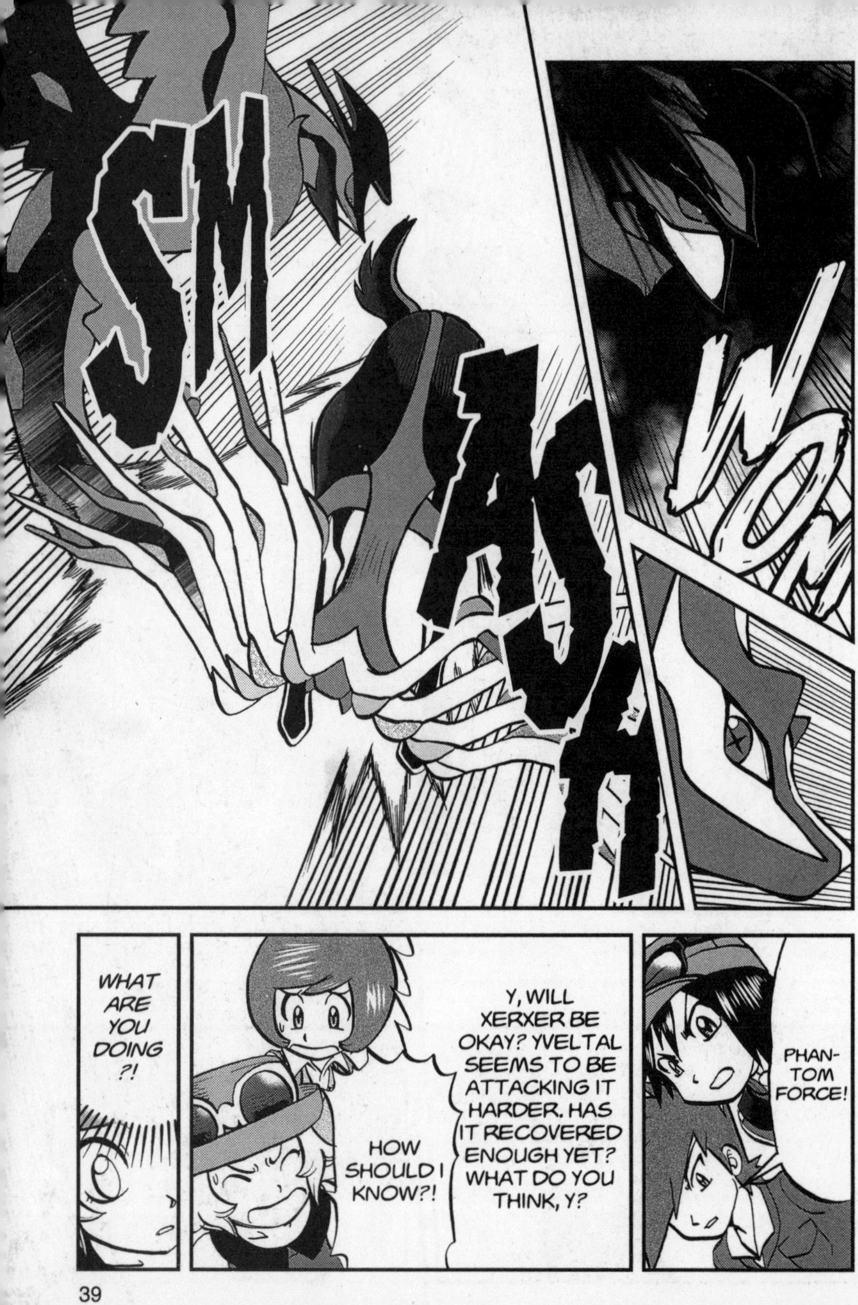
WOM
SMAAA
PHAN-TOM FORCE!
Y, WILL XERXER BE OKAY? YVELTAL SEEMS TO BE ATTACKING IT HARDER. HAS IT RECOVERED ENOUGH YET? WHAT DO YOU THINK, Y?
HOW SHOULD I KNOW?!
WHAT ARE YOU DOING ?!

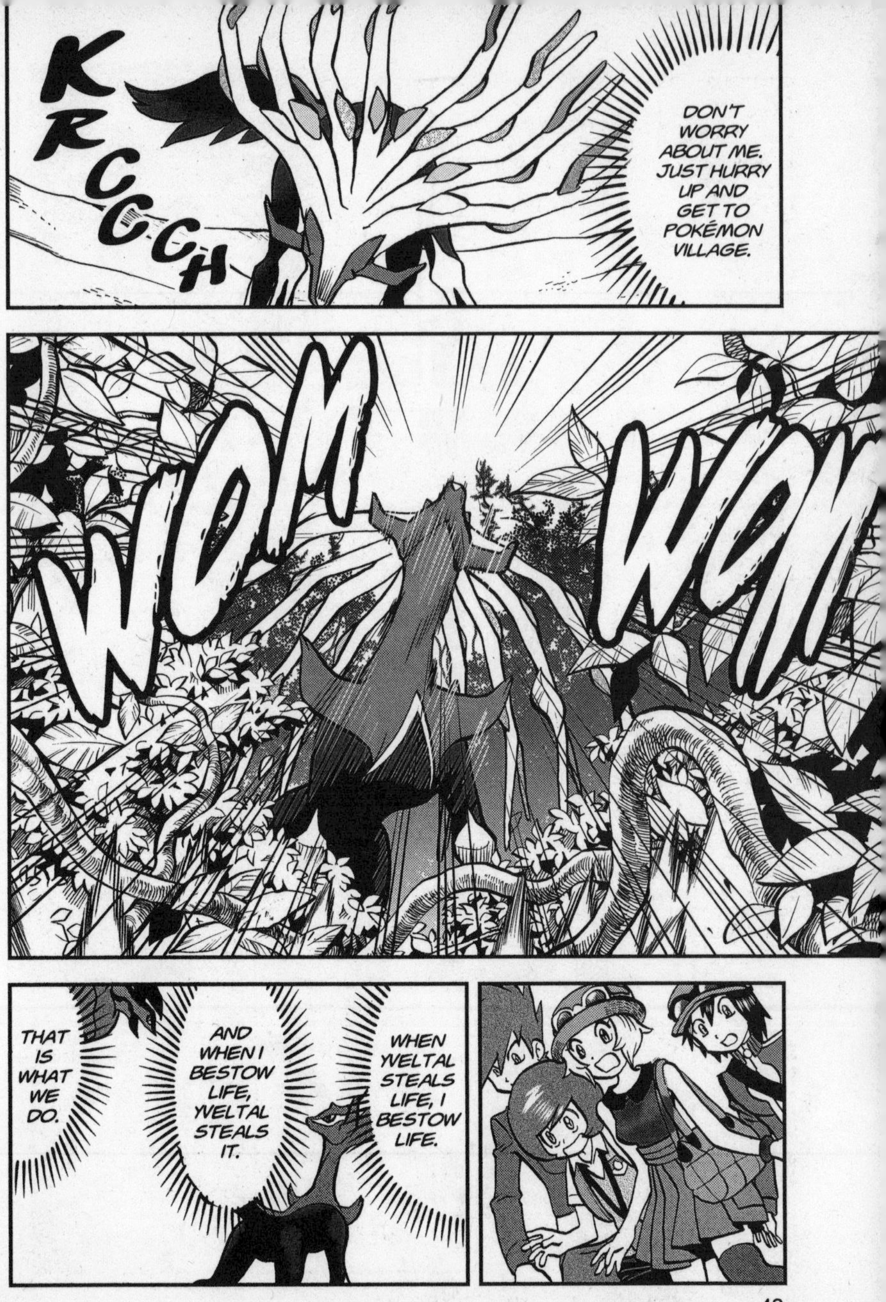
DON'T WORRY ABOUT ME. JUST HURRY UP AND GET TO POKÉMON VILLAGE.
KRCCCH
WOM
WOM
WHEN YVELTAL STEALS LIFE, I BESTOW LIFE.
AND WHEN I BESTOW LIFE, YVELTAL STEALS IT.
THAT IS WHAT WE DO.

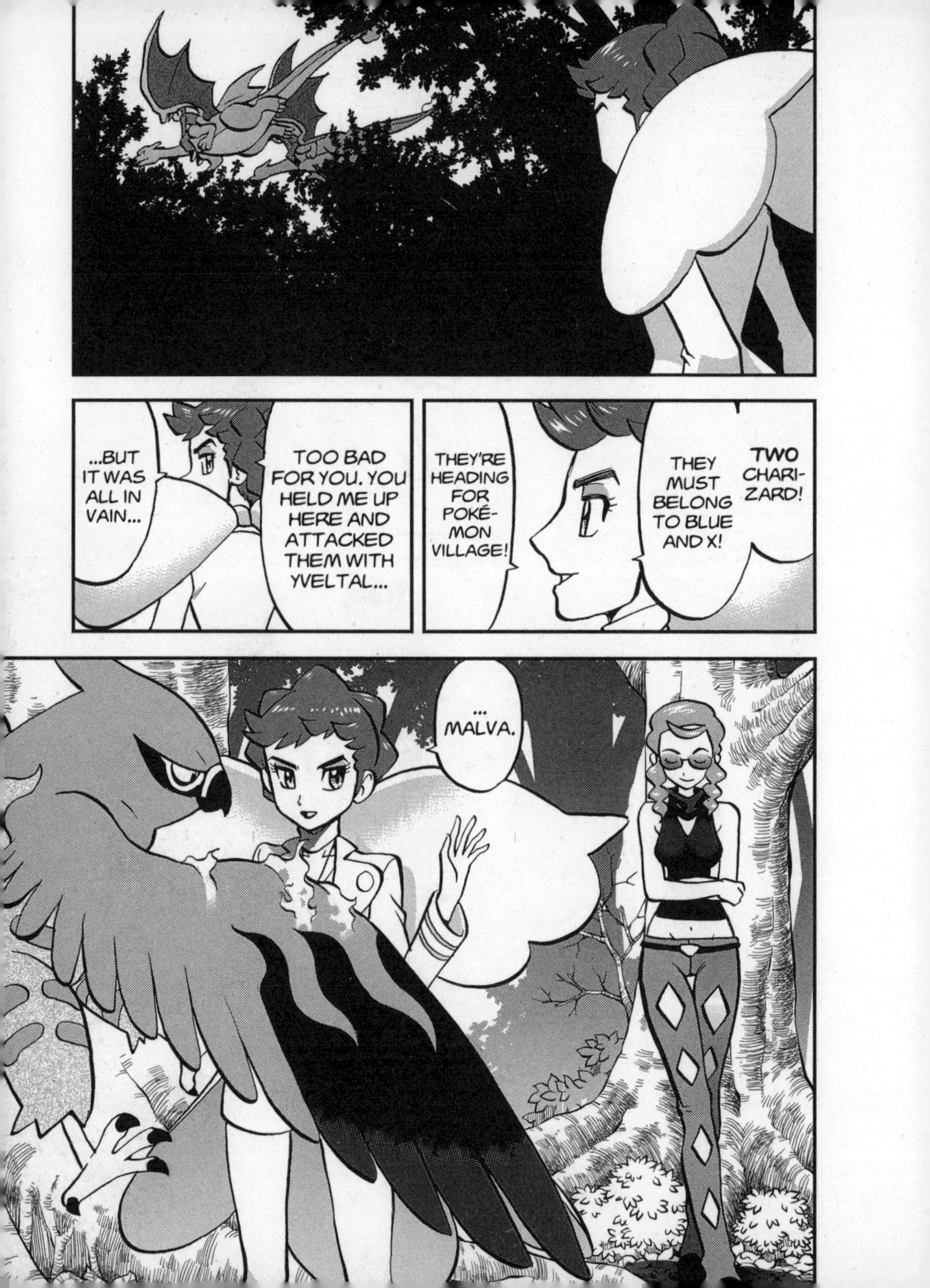
TWO CHARIZARD!
THEY MUST BELONG TO BLUE AND X!
THEY'RE HEADING FOR POKÉMON VILLAGE!
TOO BAD FOR YOU. YOU HELD ME UP HERE AND ATTACKED THEM WITH YVELTAL...
...BUT IT WAS ALL IN VAIN...
... MALVA.

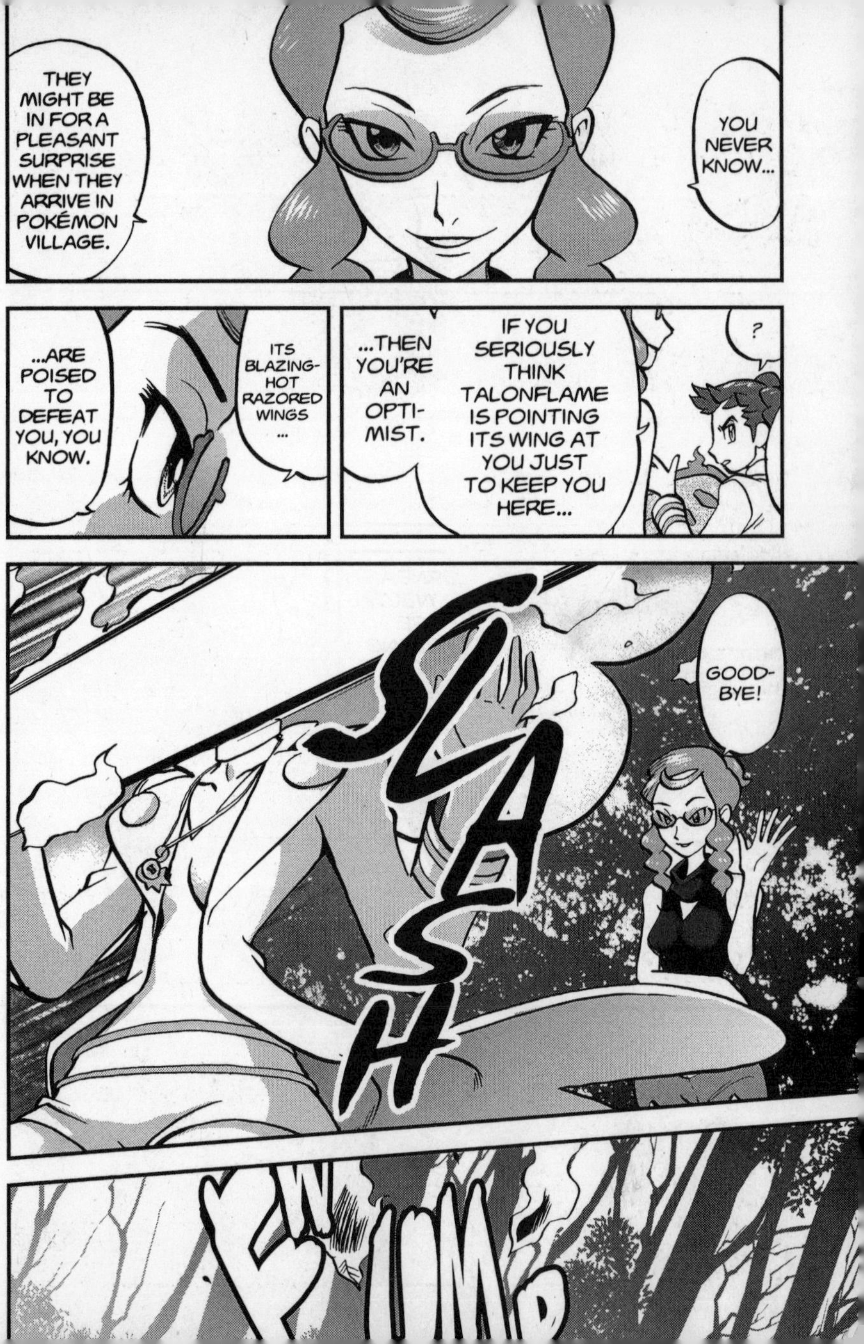
THEY MIGHT BE IN FOR A PLEASANT SURPRISE WHEN THEY ARRIVE IN POKÉMON VILLAGE.
YOU NEVER KNOW...
?
IF YOU SERIOUSLY THINK TALONFLAME IS POINTING ITS WING AT YOU JUST TO KEEP YOU HERE...
...THEN YOU'RE AN OPTI-MIST.
ITS BLAZING-HOT RAZORED WINGS ...
...ARE POISED TO DEFEAT YOU, YOU KNOW.
SLASH
GOOD-BYE!

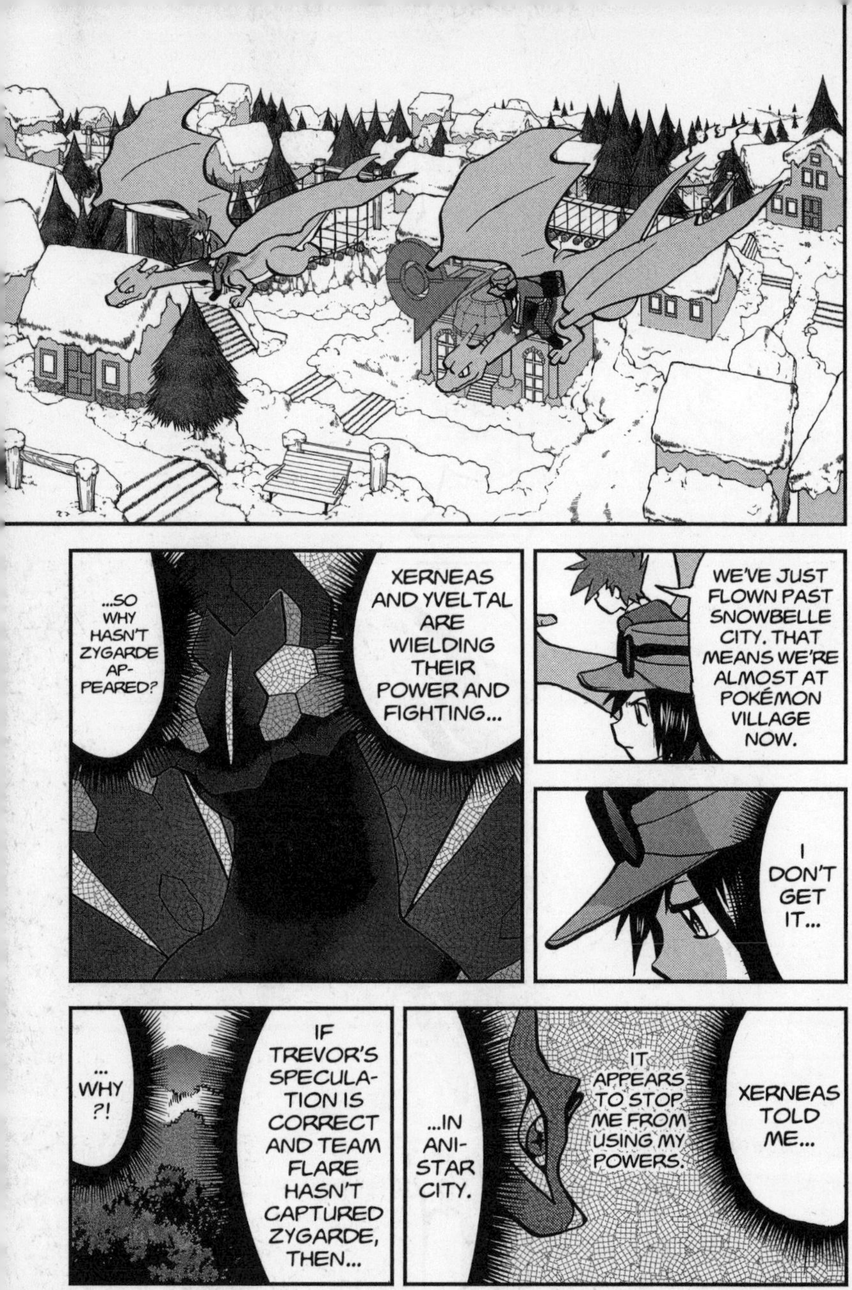
WE'VE JUST FLOWN PAST SNOWBELLE CITY. THAT MEANS WE'RE ALMOST AT POKÉMON VILLAGE NOW.
I DON'T GET IT...
XERNEAS AND YVELTAL ARE WIELDING THEIR POWER AND FIGHTING...
...SO WHY HASN'T ZYGARDE AP-PEARED?
XERNEAS TOLD ME...
IT APPEARS TO STOP ME FROM USING MY POWERS.
...IN ANI-STAR CITY.
IF TREVOR'S SPECULA-TION IS CORRECT AND TEAM FLARE HASN'T CAPTURED ZYGARDE, THEN...
... WHY ?!

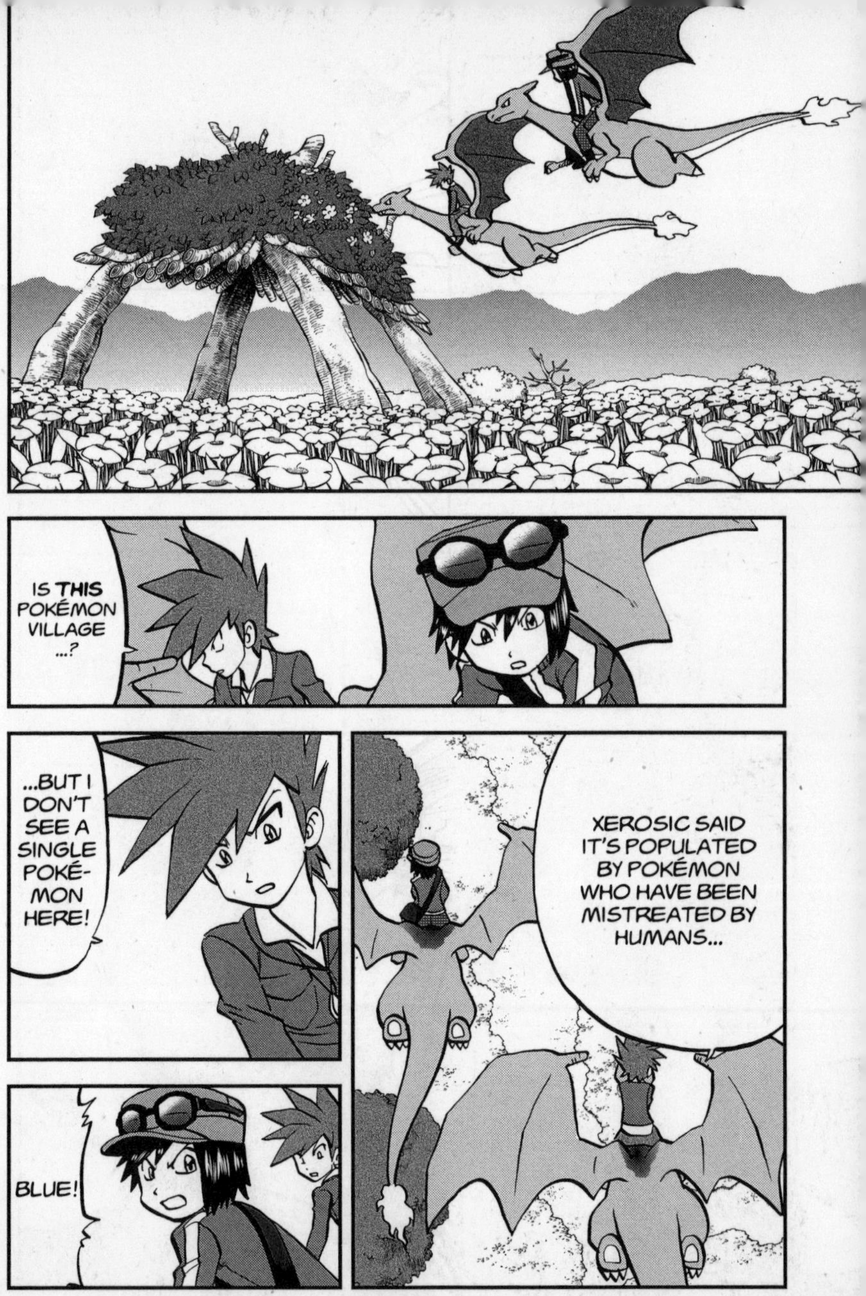
IS THIS POKÉMON VILLAGE ...?
XEROSIC SAID IT'S POPULATED BY POKÉMON WHO HAVE BEEN MISTREATED BY HUMANS...
...BUT I DON'T SEE A SINGLE POKÉ-MON HERE!
BLUE!

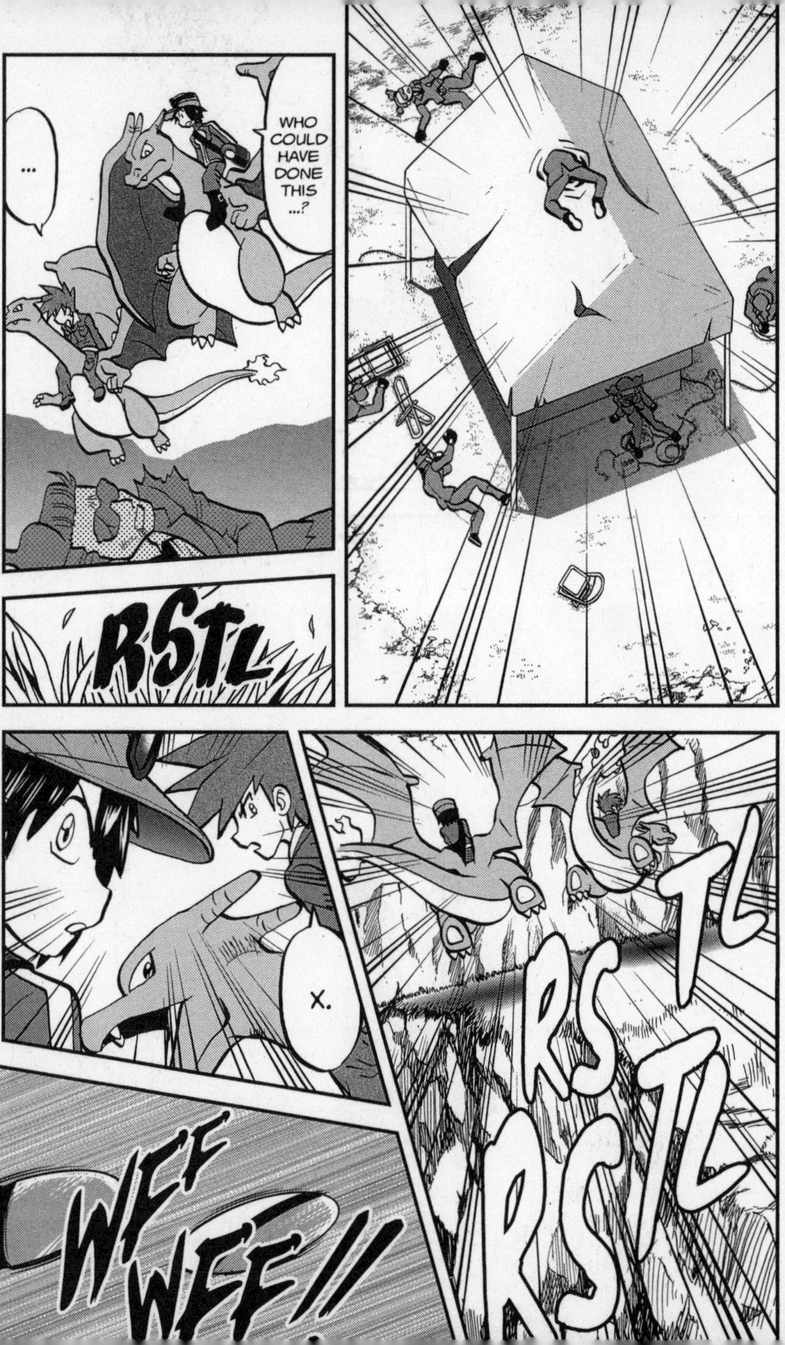
WHO COULD HAVE DONE THIS ...?
...
RSTL
RSTL
RSTL
RSTL
X.
WFF WFF!!

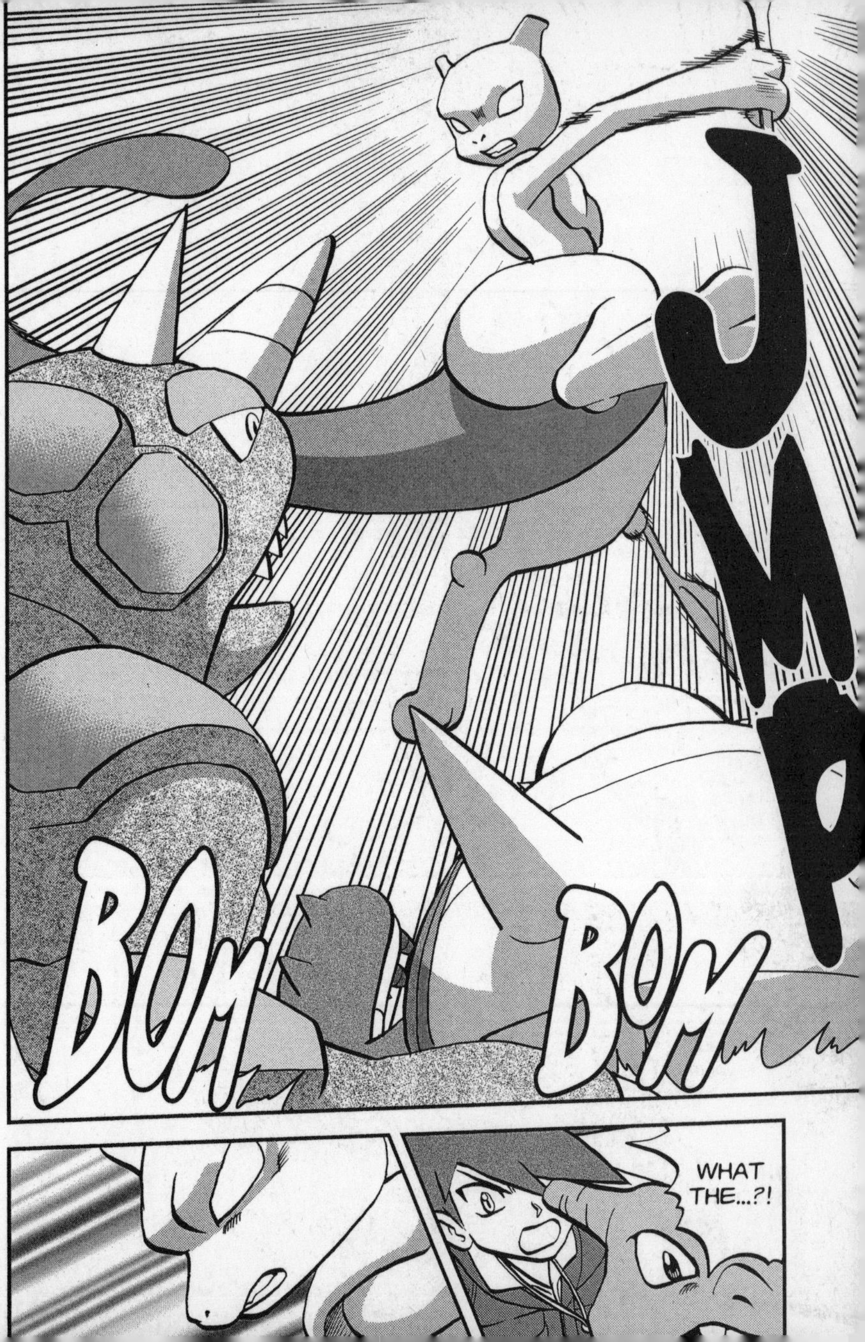
JUMP
BOM
BOM
WHAT THE...?!

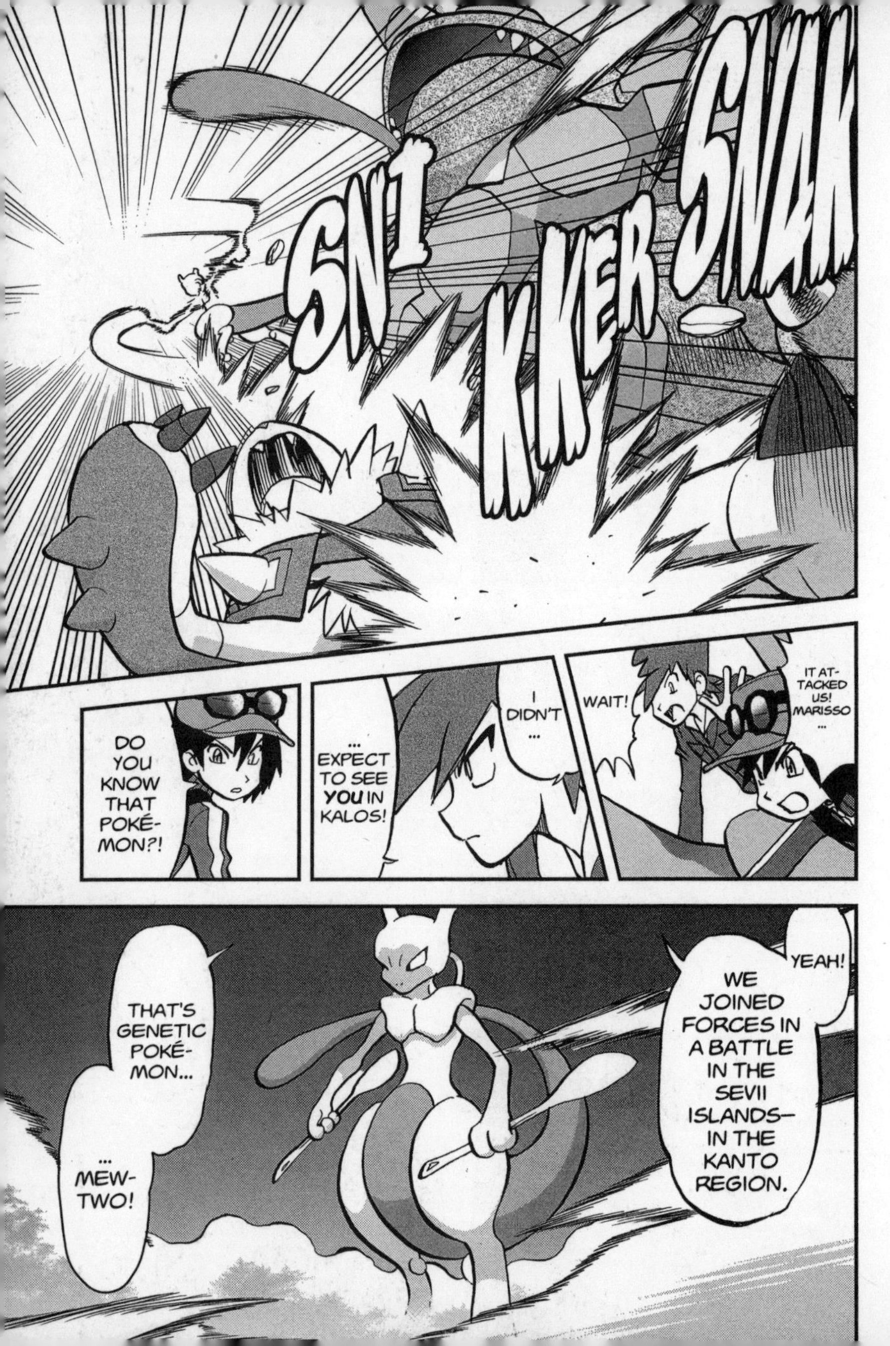
SNIKKER SNAK
IT AT-TACKED US! MARISSO ...
WAIT!
I DIDN'T ...
... EXPECT TO SEE YOU IN KALOS!
DO YOU KNOW THAT POKÉ-MON?!
YEAH!
WE JOINED FORCES IN A BATTLE IN THE SEVII ISLANDS— IN THE KANTO REGION.
THAT'S GENETIC POKÉ-MON...
... MEW-TWO!

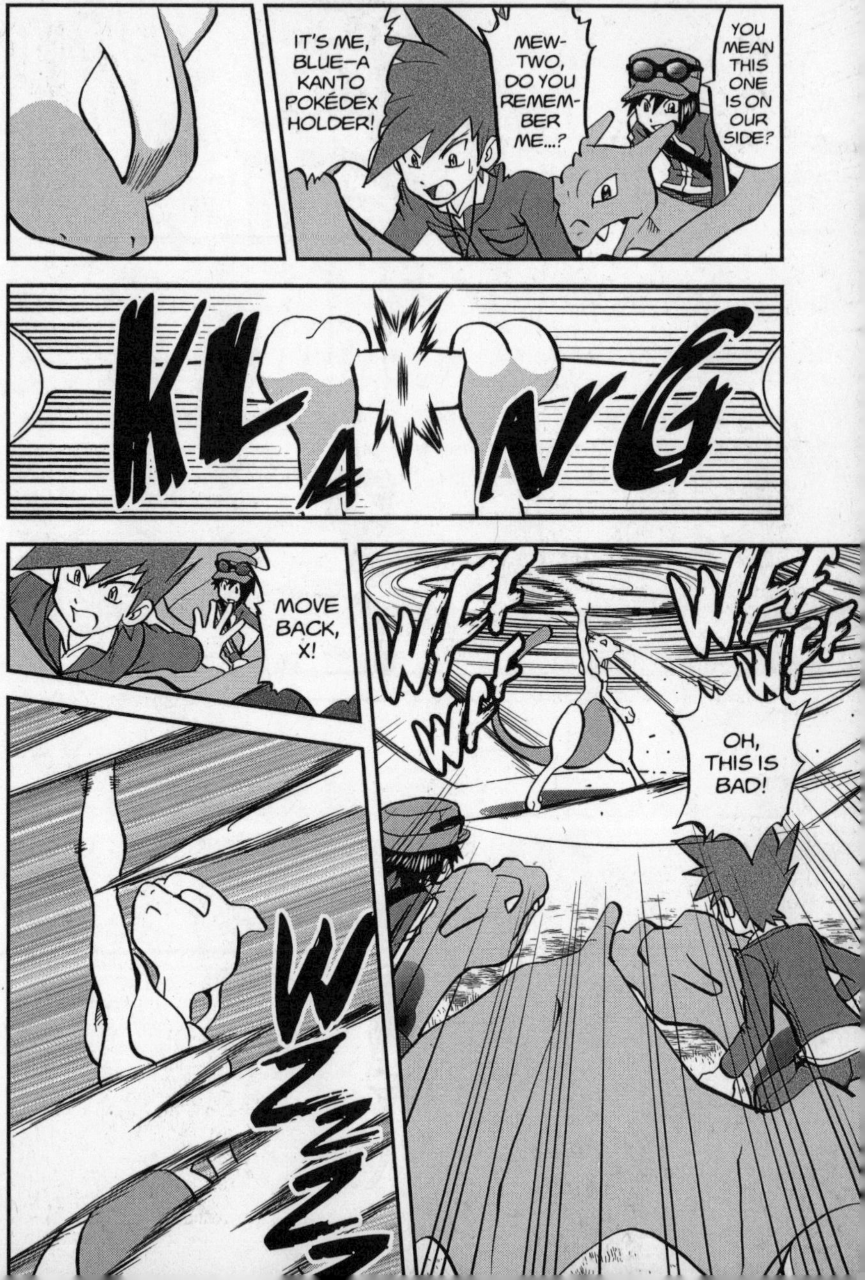
IT'S ME, BLUE—A KANTO POKÉDEX HOLDER!
MEW-TWO, DO YOU REMEMBER ME...?
YOU MEAN THIS ONE IS ON OUR SIDE?
KLANG
MOVE BACK, X!
WFF WFF WFF WFF
OH, THIS IS BAD!
WZZ

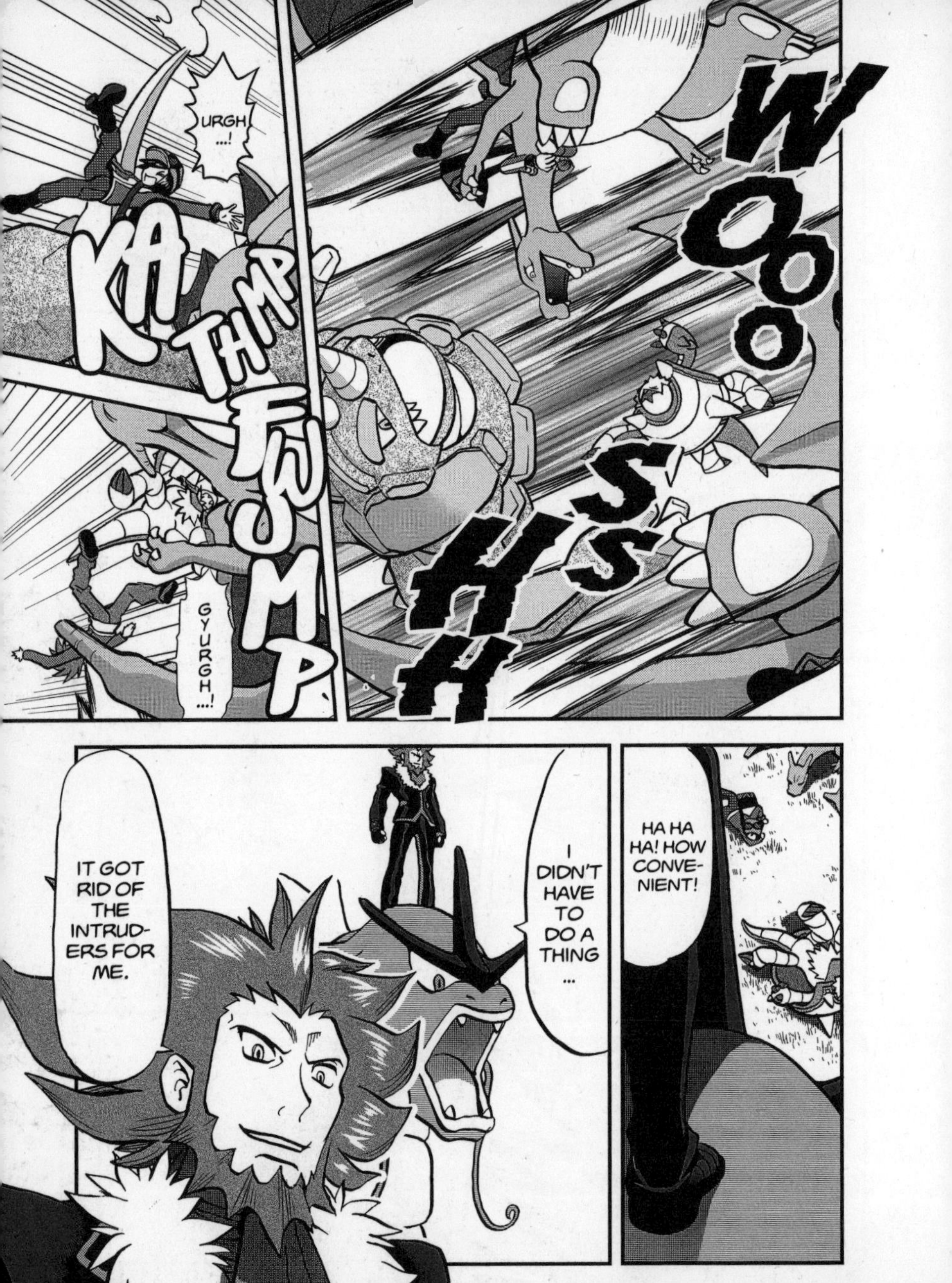
WOOO
HISS
URGH ...!
KA THMP
FWUMP
GYURGH ...!
HA HA HA! HOW CONVE-NIENT!
I DIDN'T HAVE TO DO A THING ...
IT GOT RID OF THE INTRUD-ERS FOR ME.

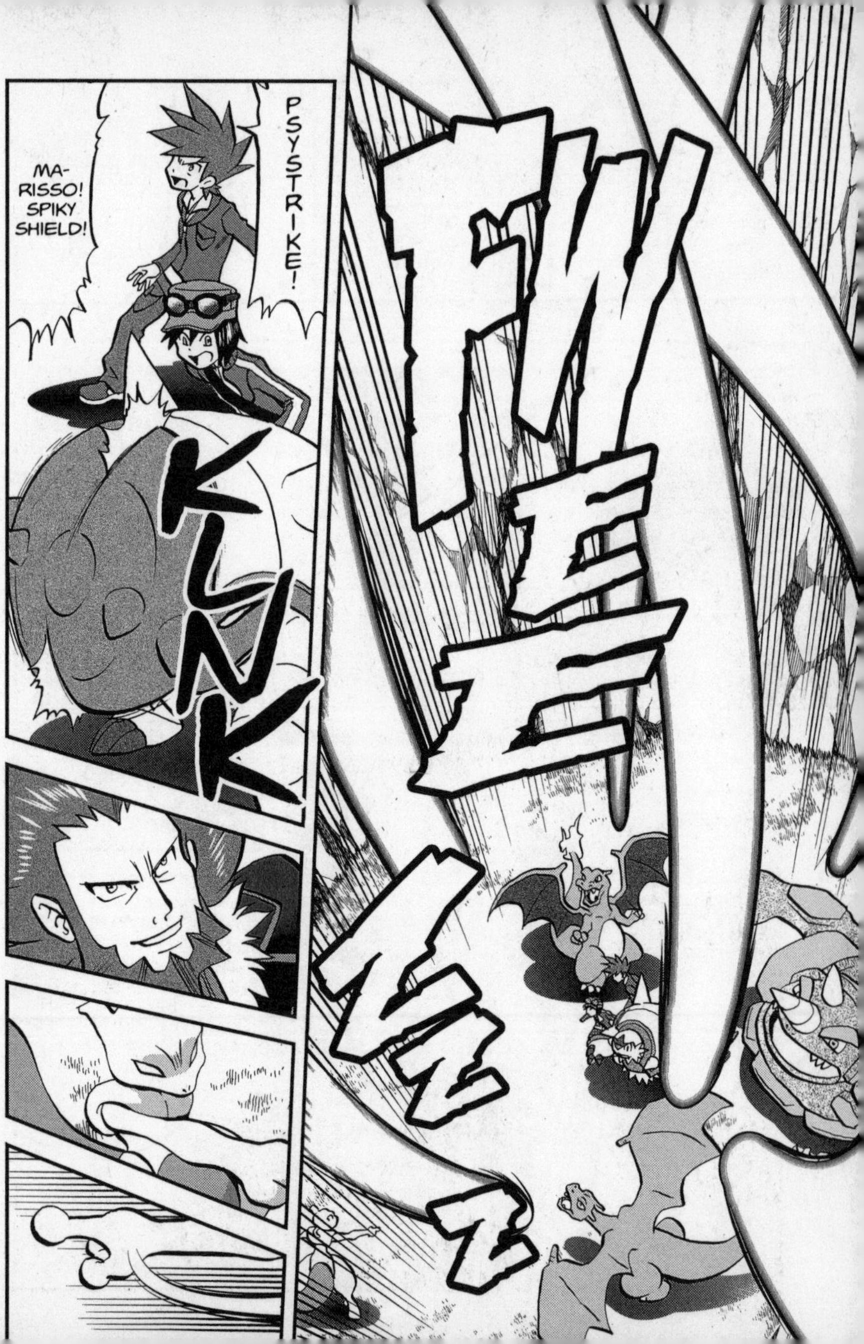
PSYSTRIKE!
MA-RISSO! SPIKY SHIELD!

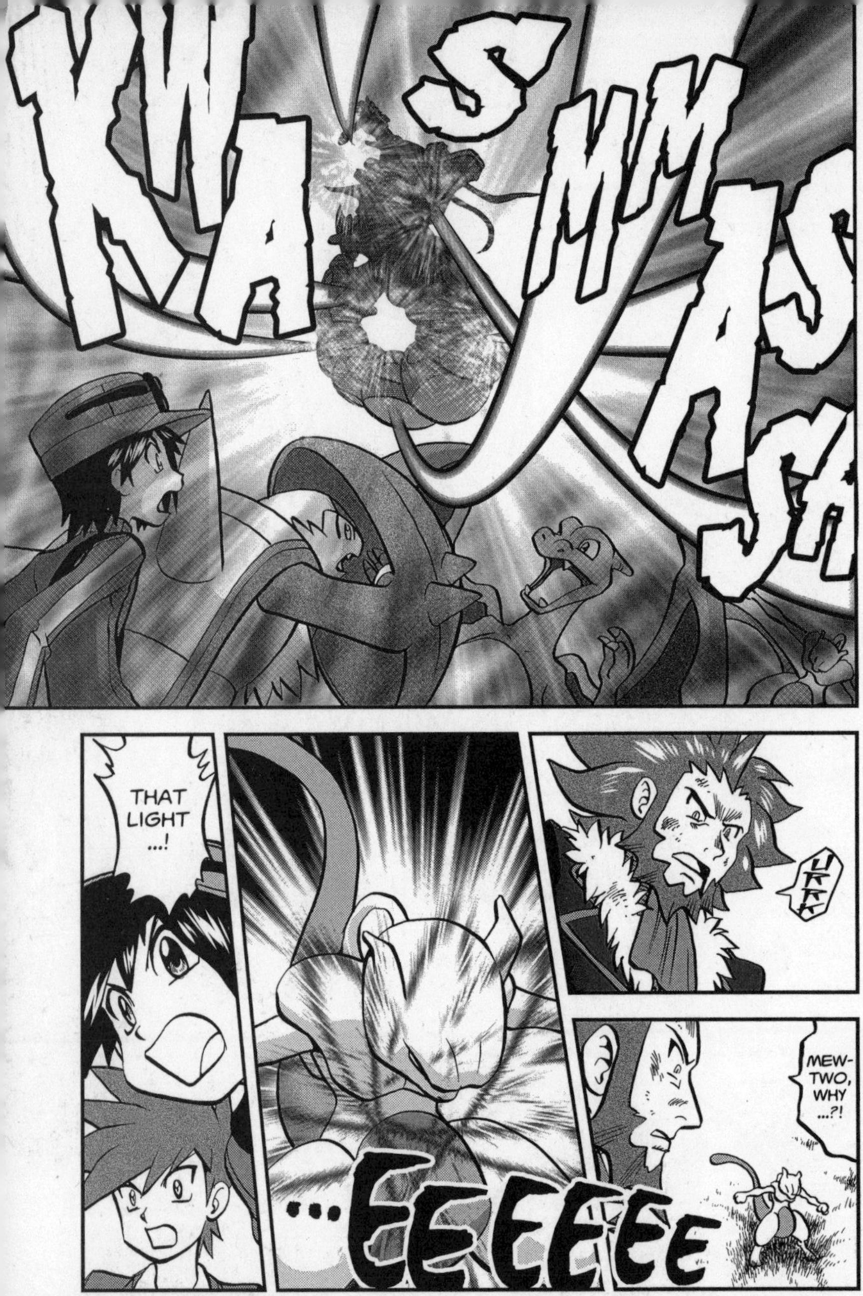
KWA
SMMASH
URRK
MEW-TWO, WHY ...?!
...EEEEEE
THAT LIGHT ...!

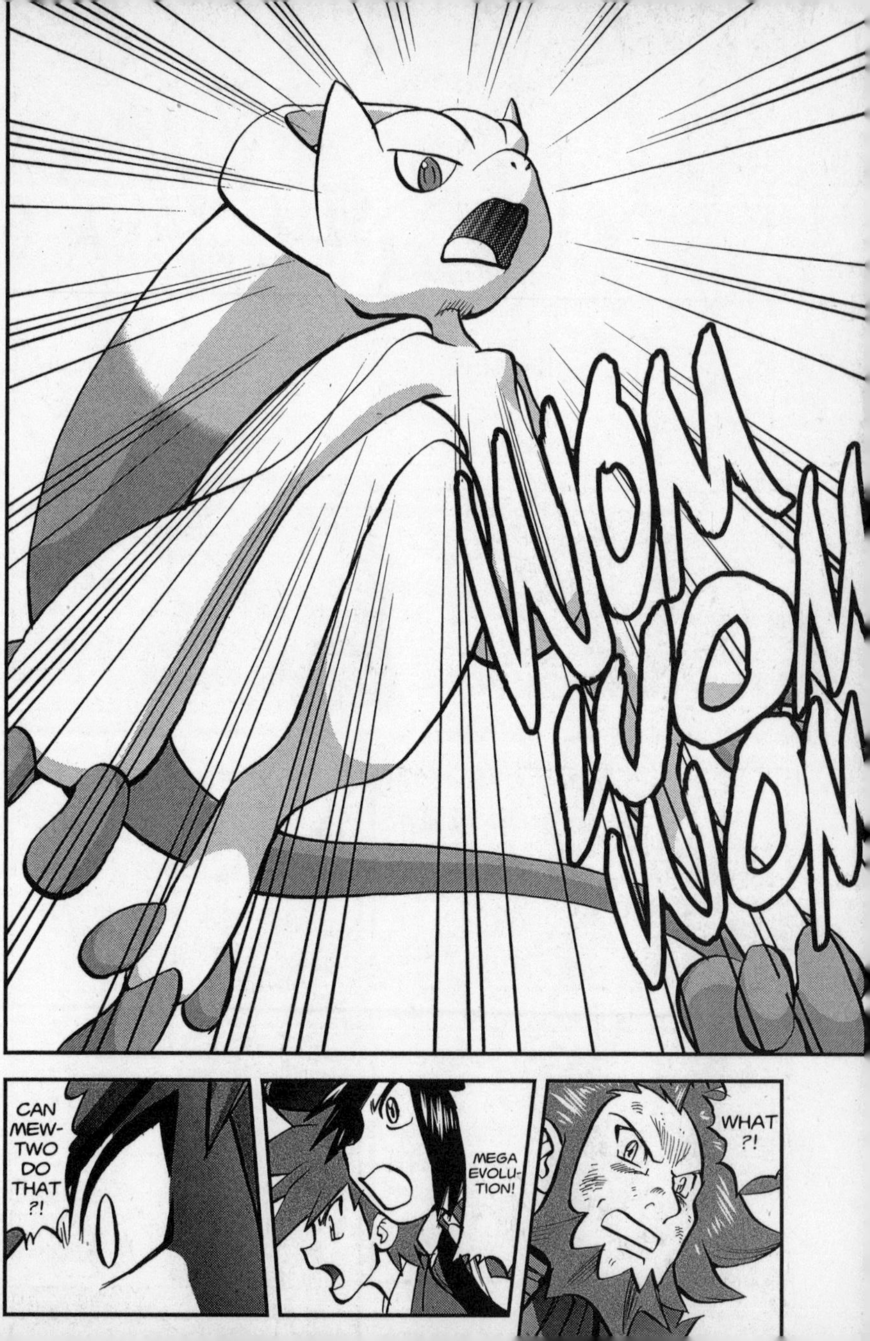
WWOM WWOM WWOM
WHAT ?!
MEGA EVOLU- TION!
CAN MEW- TWO DO THAT ?!

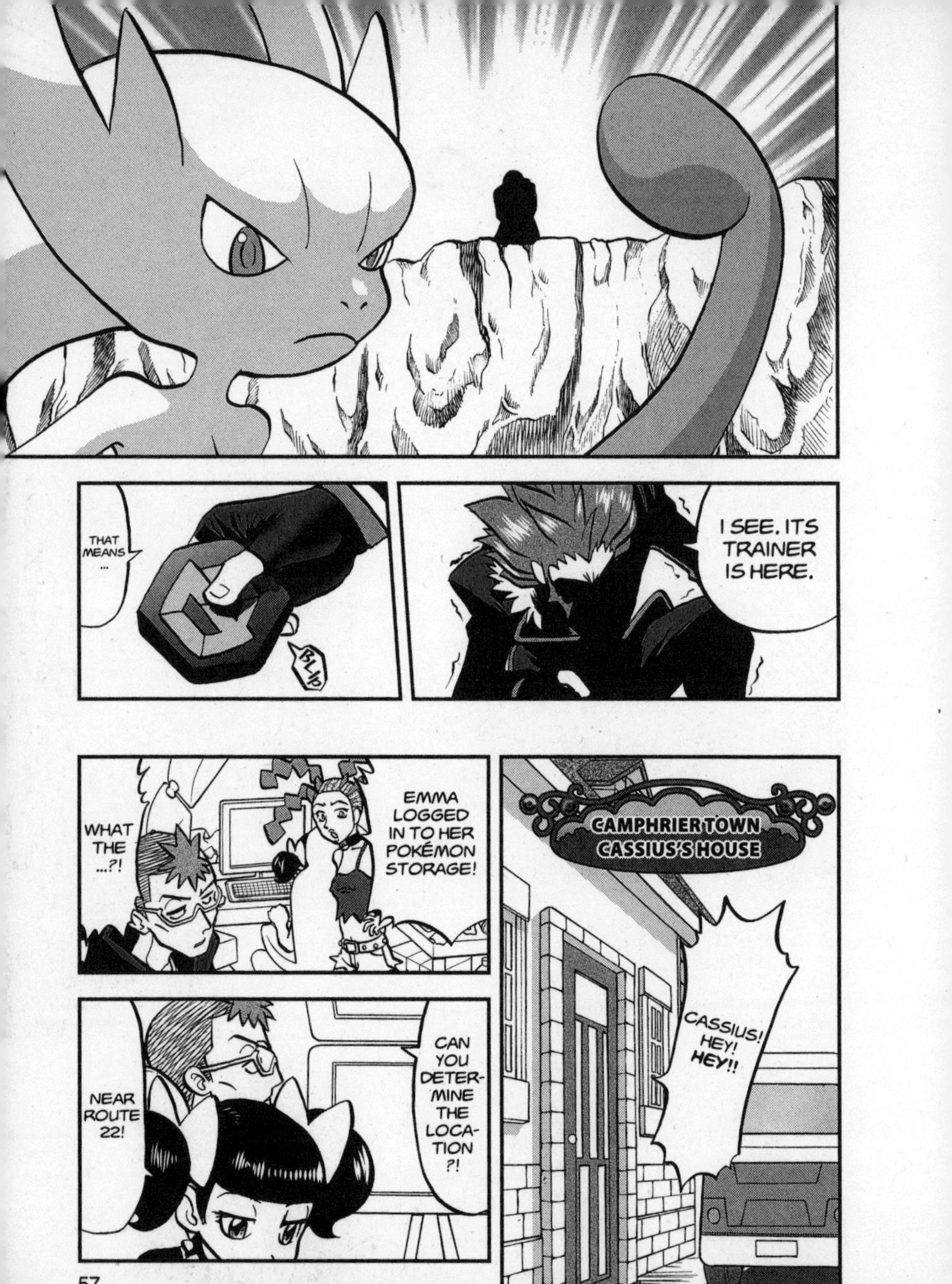
I SEE. ITS TRAINER IS HERE.
THAT MEANS ...
BLIP
CAMPHRIER TOWN CASSIUS'S HOUSE
CASSIUS! HEY! HEY!!
EMMA LOGGED IN TO HER POKÉMON STORAGE!
WHAT THE ...?!
CAN YOU DETER-MINE THE LOCA-TION ?!
NEAR ROUTE 22!

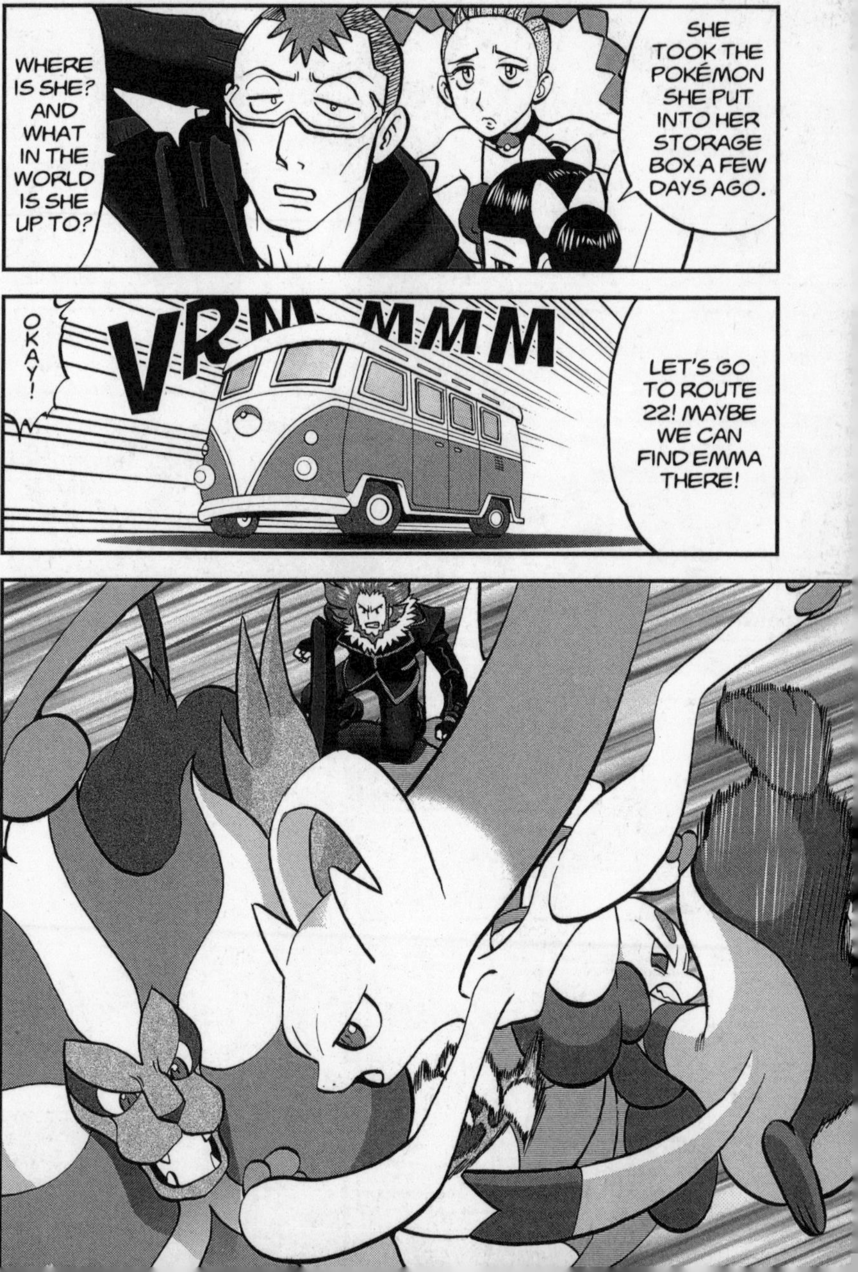
SHE TOOK THE POKÉMON SHE PUT INTO HER STORAGE BOX A FEW DAYS AGO.
WHERE IS SHE? AND WHAT IN THE WORLD IS SHE UP TO?
LET'S GO TO ROUTE 22! MAYBE WE CAN FIND EMMA THERE!
VRM MMMM
OKAY!

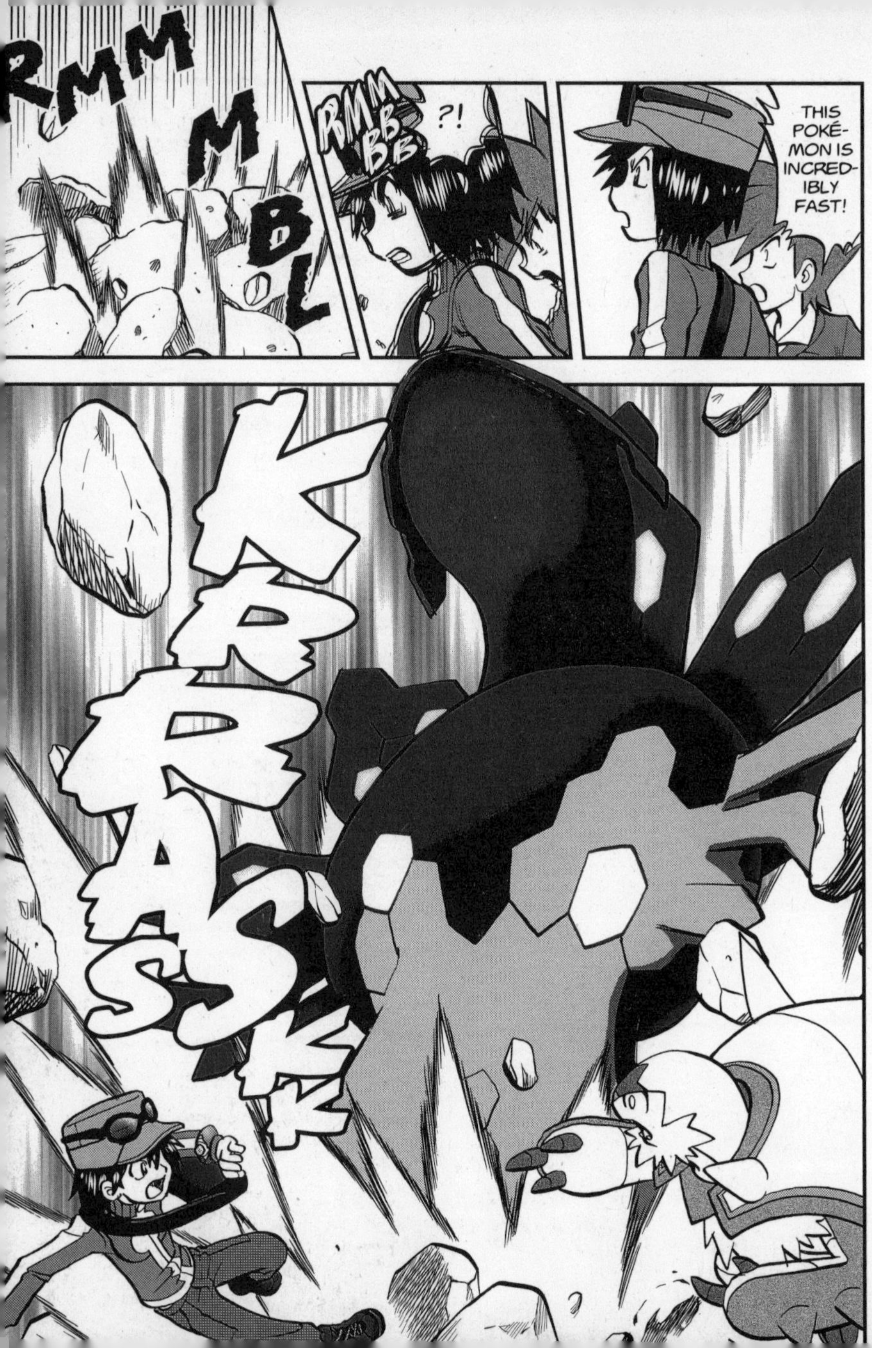
THIS POKÉMON IS INCREDIBLY FAST!
RMM BBBB
?!
RMMMBL
KRRASSK

Current Location

Route 18
Vallée Étroite Way

This path is best known for its
trolley, once used for the coal
mine, and the curious Inverse
Battle House.

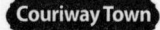

Couriway Town

The railway brings people from
great distances to see the huge,
majestic falls.

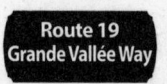

Route 19
Grande Vallée Way

This great valley can now be
crossed thanks to its long
bridge, built with the help of
many Pokémon.

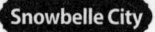

Snowbelle City

They say the cold air flowing from
the Pokémon Gym is responsible
for this city's frozen state.

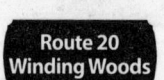

Route 20
Winding Woods

This path was designed to disturb
the woods as little as possible,
so it twists and turns among
the trees.

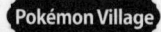

Pokémon Village

Legends say a place exists where
Pokémon live in hiding, but no
one has ever found it.

Adventure 36 Mewtwo Angered

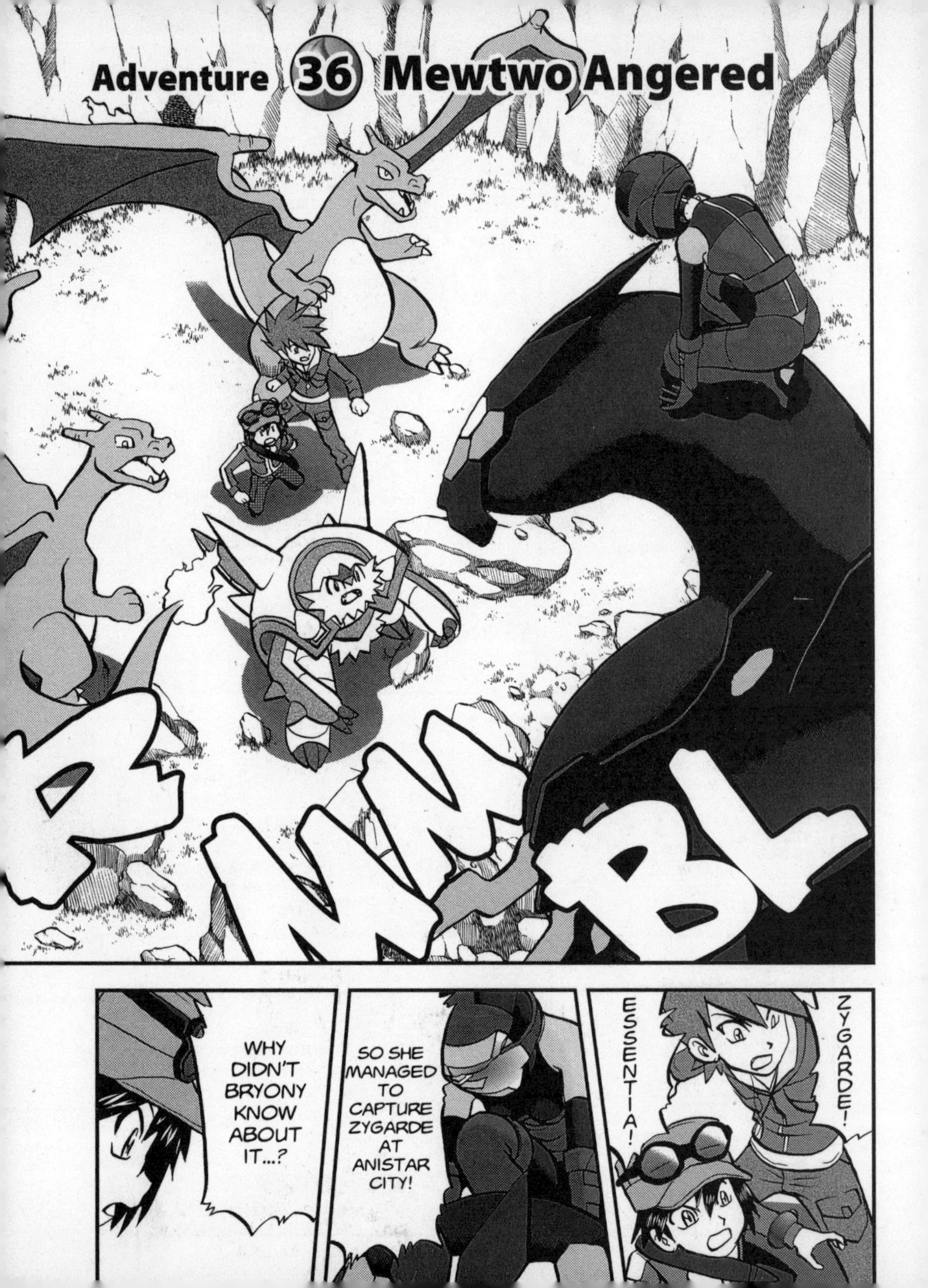
ZYGARDE!
ESSENTIA!
SO SHE MANAGED TO CAPTURE ZYGARDE AT ANISTAR CITY!
WHY DIDN'T BRYONY KNOW ABOUT IT...?

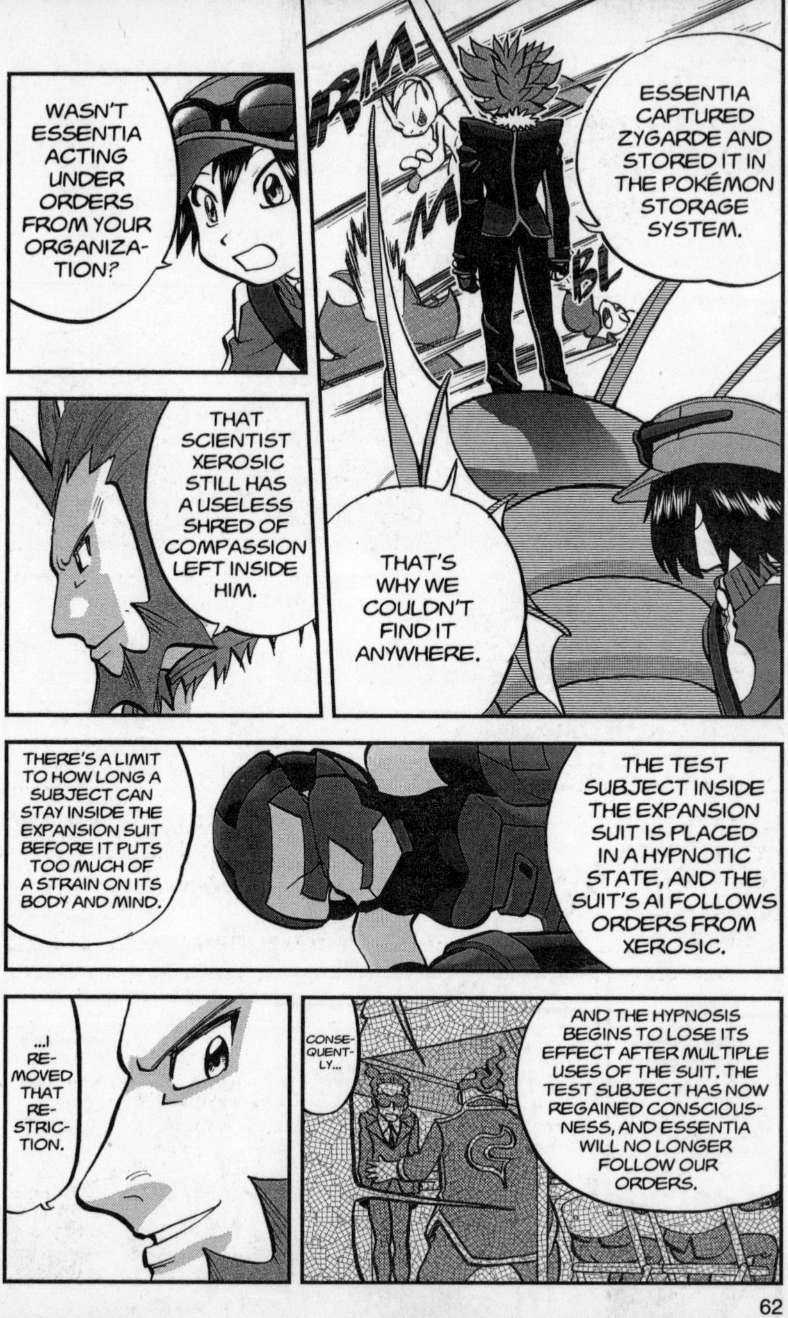

VRRMMMMBL
ESSENTIA CAPTURED ZYGARDE AND STORED IT IN THE POKÉMON STORAGE SYSTEM.
THAT'S WHY WE COULDN'T FIND IT ANYWHERE.
WASN'T ESSENTIA ACTING UNDER ORDERS FROM YOUR ORGANIZA-TION?
THAT SCIENTIST XEROSIC STILL HAS A USELESS SHRED OF COMPASSION LEFT INSIDE HIM.
THE TEST SUBJECT INSIDE THE EXPANSION SUIT IS PLACED IN A HYPNOTIC STATE, AND THE SUIT'S AI FOLLOWS ORDERS FROM XEROSIC.
THERE'S A LIMIT TO HOW LONG A SUBJECT CAN STAY INSIDE THE EXPANSION SUIT BEFORE IT PUTS TOO MUCH OF A STRAIN ON ITS BODY AND MIND.
AND THE HYPNOSIS BEGINS TO LOSE ITS EFFECT AFTER MULTIPLE USES OF THE SUIT. THE TEST SUBJECT HAS NOW REGAINED CONSCIOUS-NESS, AND ESSENTIA WILL NO LONGER FOLLOW OUR ORDERS.
CONSE-QUENT-LY...
...I RE-MOVED THAT RE-STRIC-TION.

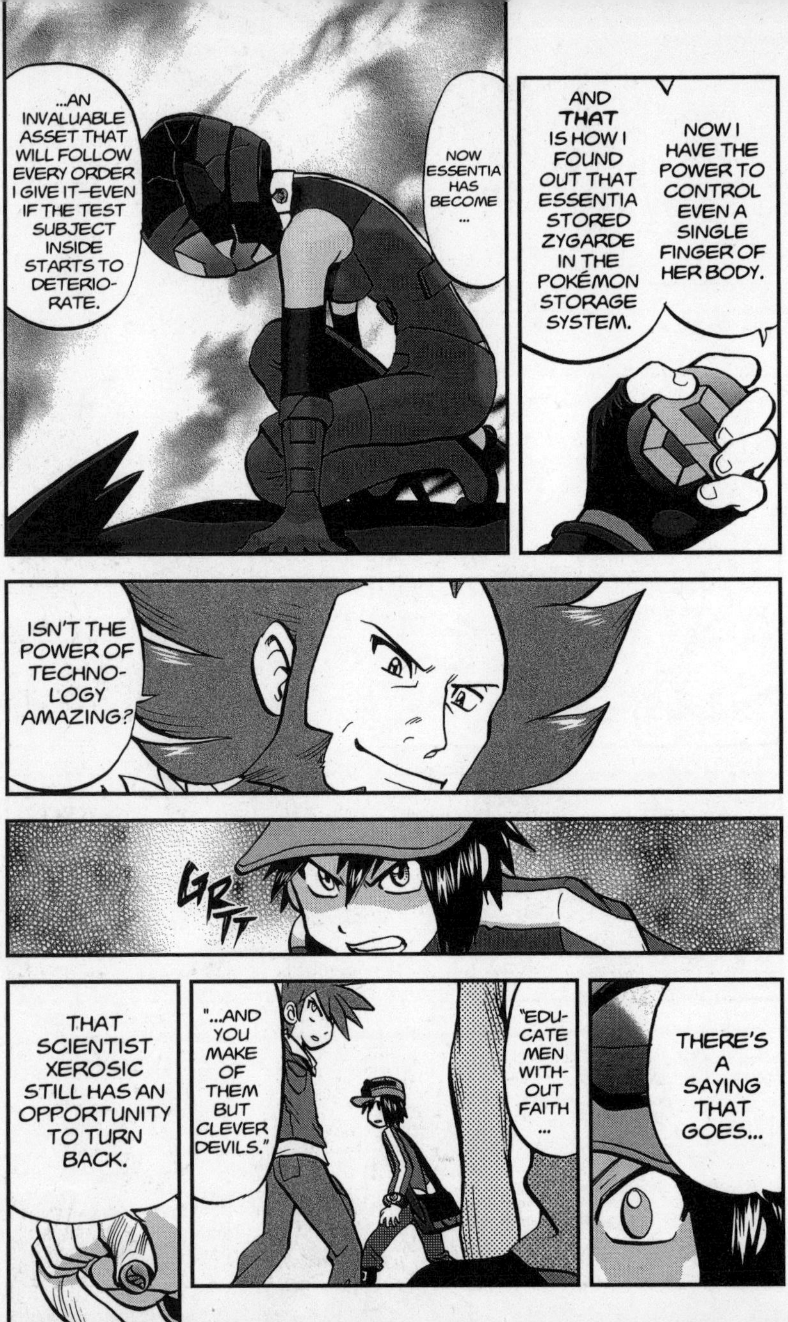
AND THAT IS HOW I FOUND OUT THAT ESSENTIA STORED ZYGARDE IN THE POKÉMON STORAGE SYSTEM.
NOW I HAVE THE POWER TO CONTROL EVEN A SINGLE FINGER OF HER BODY.
NOW ESSENTIA HAS BECOME ...
...AN INVALUABLE ASSET THAT WILL FOLLOW EVERY ORDER I GIVE IT—EVEN IF THE TEST SUBJECT INSIDE STARTS TO DETERIO-RATE.
ISN'T THE POWER OF TECHNO-LOGY AMAZING?
GRTT
THERE'S A SAYING THAT GOES...
"EDU-CATE MEN WITH-OUT FAITH ...
"...AND YOU MAKE OF THEM BUT CLEVER DEVILS."
THAT SCIENTIST XEROSIC STILL HAS AN OPPORTUNITY TO TURN BACK.

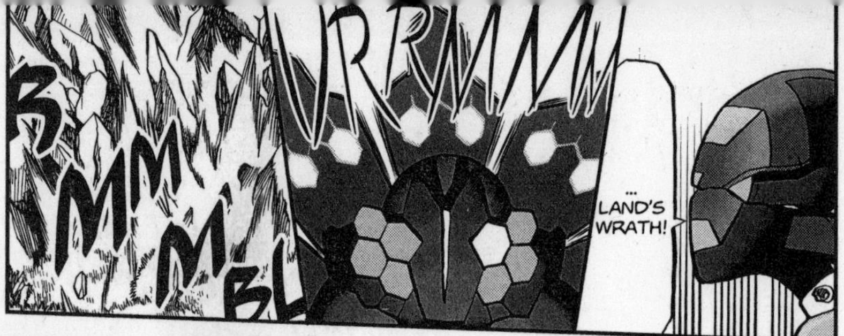
...
LAND'S
WRATH!
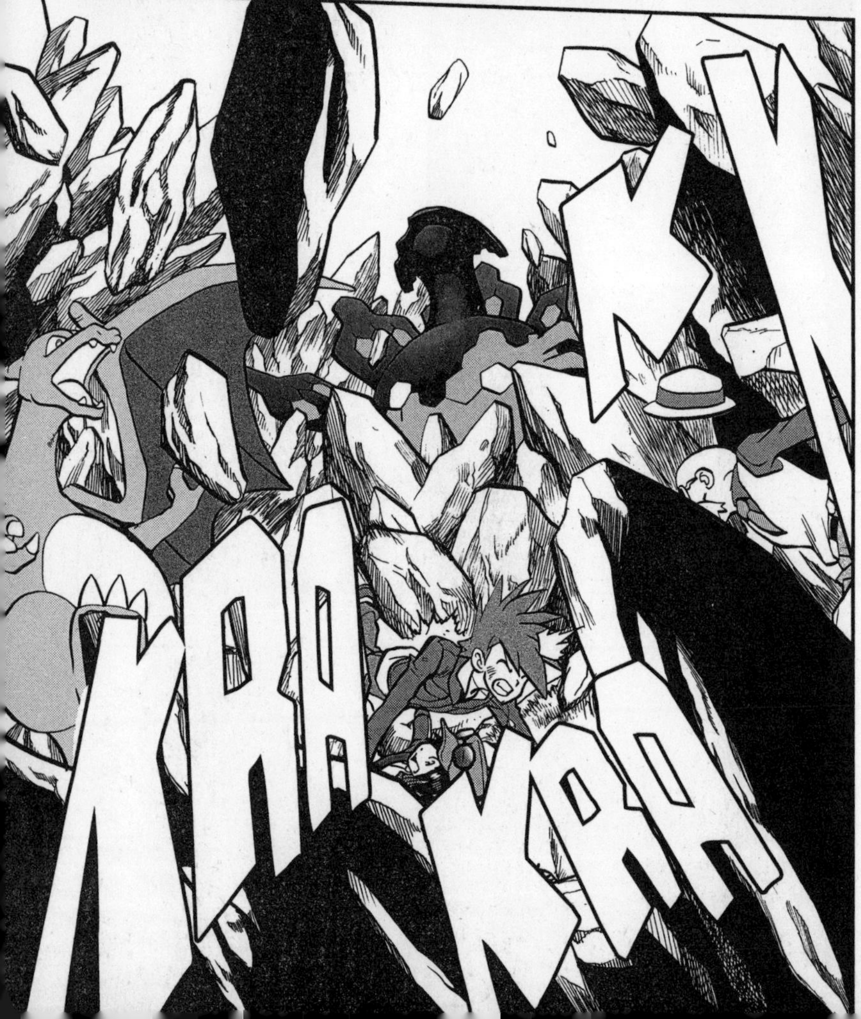

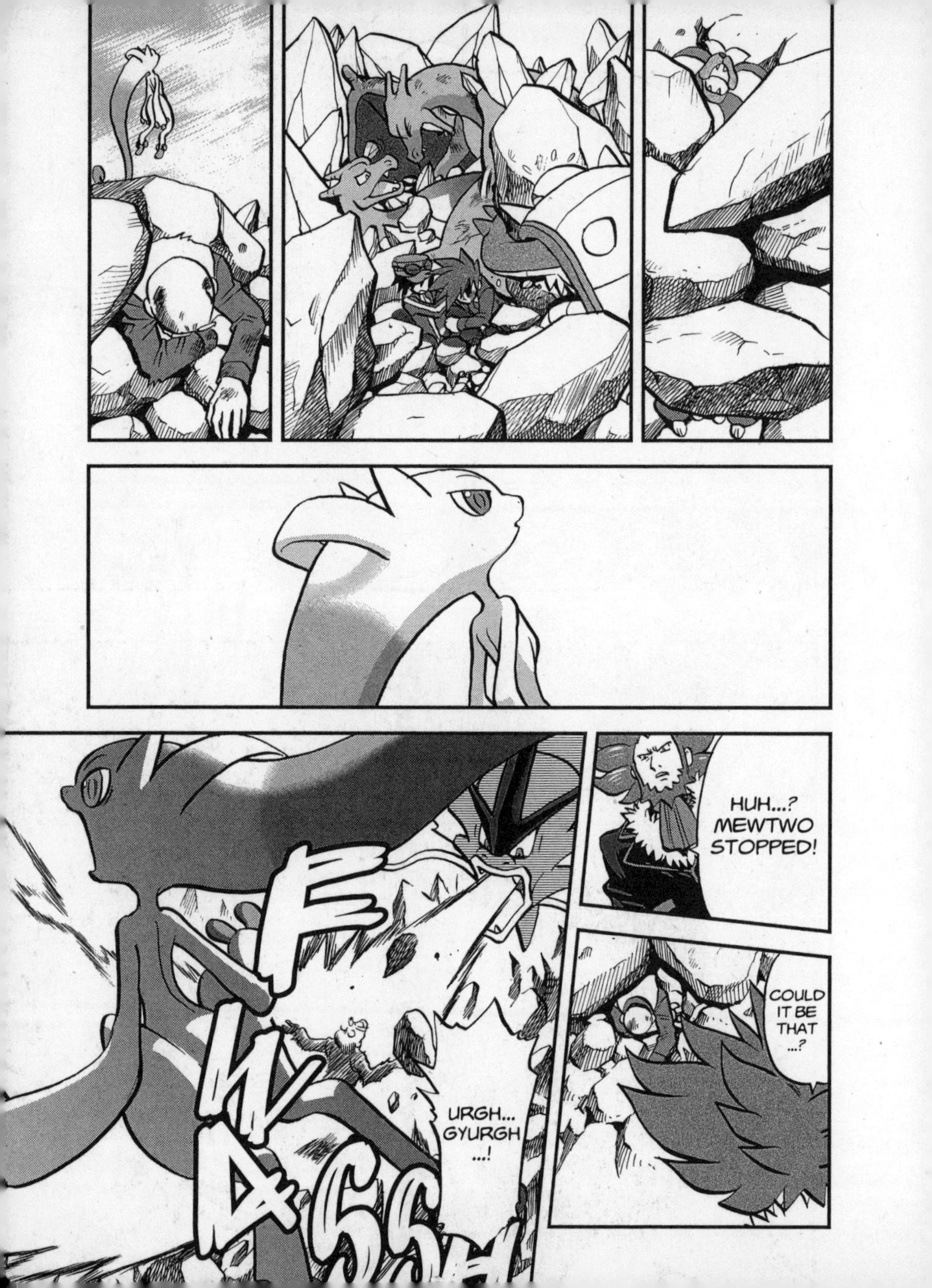
HUH...? MEWTWO STOPPED!
COULD IT BE THAT ...?
URGH... GYURGH ...!
FWASSH

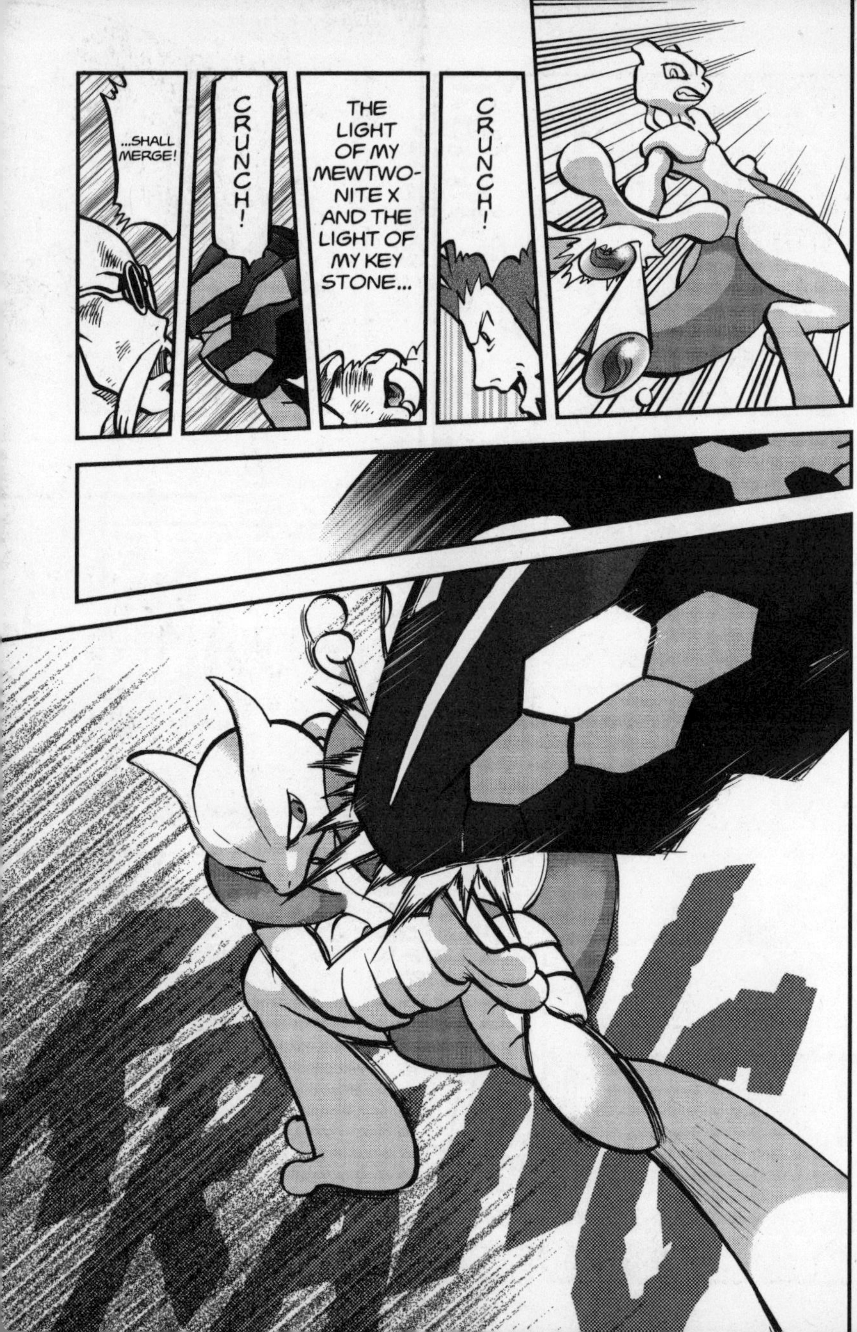
CRUNCH!
THE LIGHT OF MY MEWTWO-NITE X AND THE LIGHT OF MY KEY STONE...
CRUNCH!
...SHALL MERGE!

...THERE IS A PART OF ME INSIDE MY BROTHER AND A PART OF MY BROTHER THAT REMAINS INSIDE OF ME—AND THAT UNIQUE RELATIONSHIP ENABLES US TO SWITCH OUT MEWTWO'S MEGA EVOLUTION.

MEGA EVOLUTION CAN ONLY BE USED ONCE IN BATTLE WITH ONE KEY STONE. HOWEVER...

BUT IT'S THE SAME MEWTWO!

MEWTWO MEGA EVOLVED INTO A DIFFERENT FORM!

I CLEARLY HAVE THE UPPER HAND.

BUT EVEN WITH THAT POWER, THE BEST IT CAN DO IS BLOCK ITSELF FROM MY ATTACK.

A FORM OF MEGA EVOLUTION THAT SPECIALIZES IN PHYSICAL ATTACK, EH?

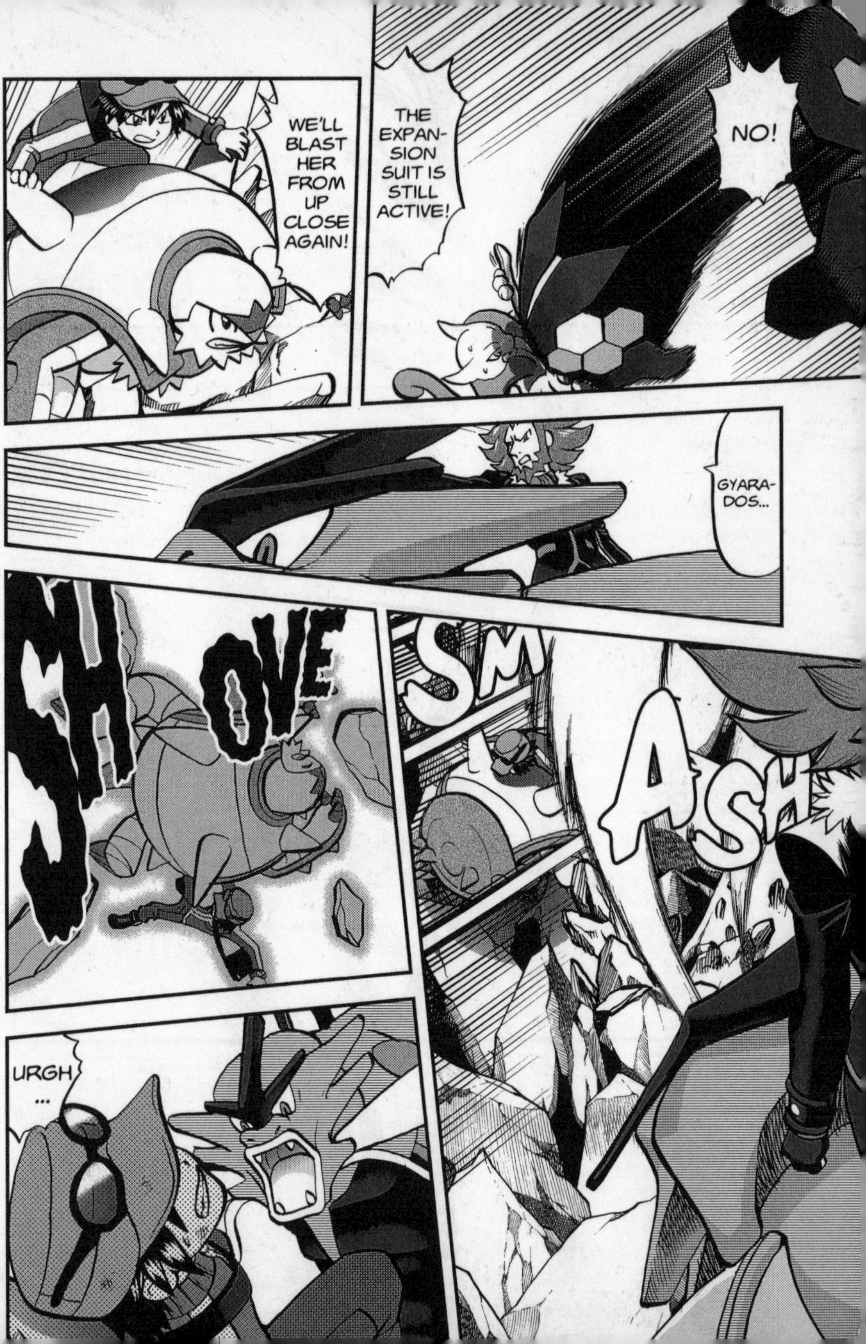
NO!
THE EXPAN-SION SUIT IS STILL ACTIVE!
WE'LL BLAST HER FROM UP CLOSE AGAIN!
GYARA-DOS...
SMASH
SHOVE
URGH...

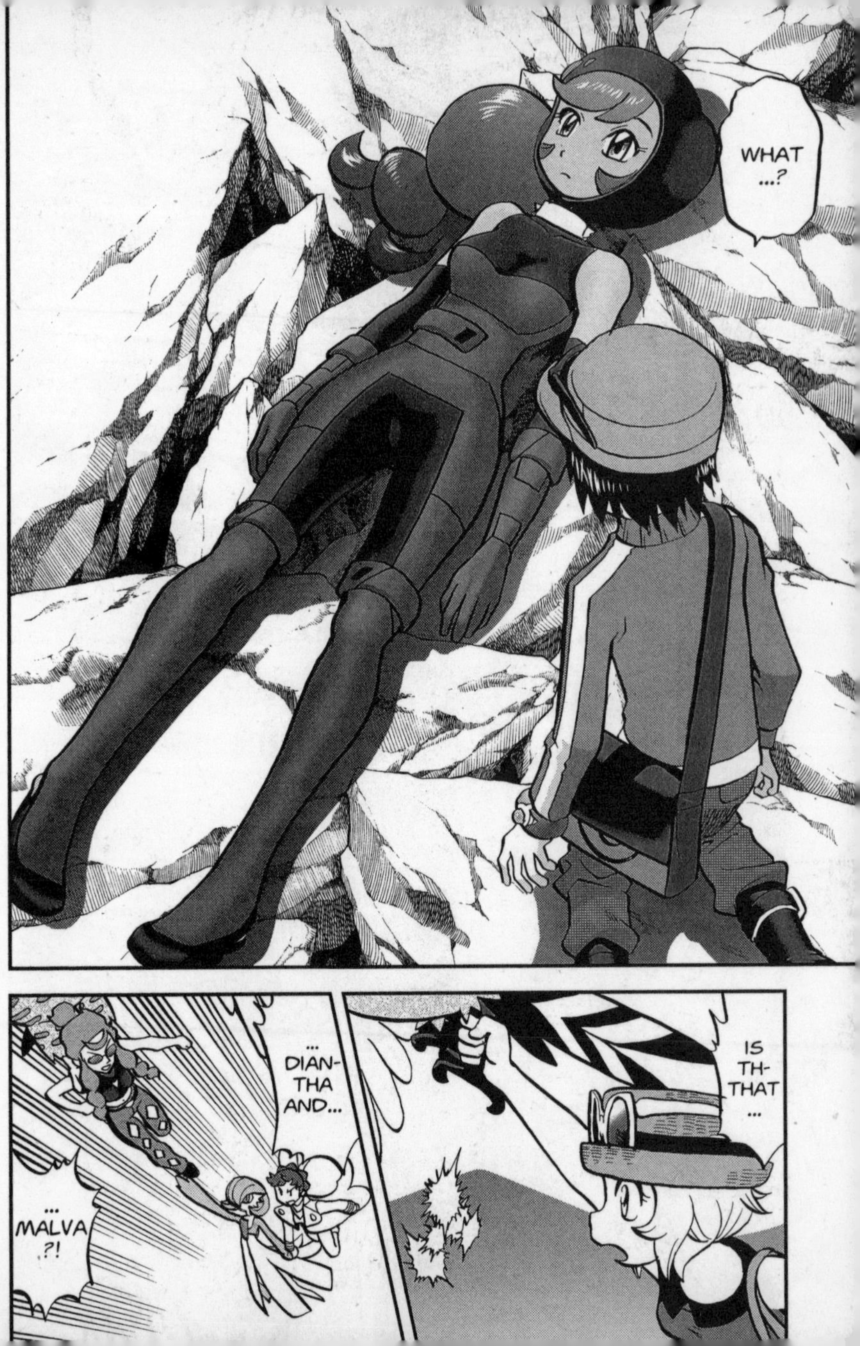
WHAT ...?
IS TH-THAT ...
... DIAN-THA AND...
... MALVA ?!

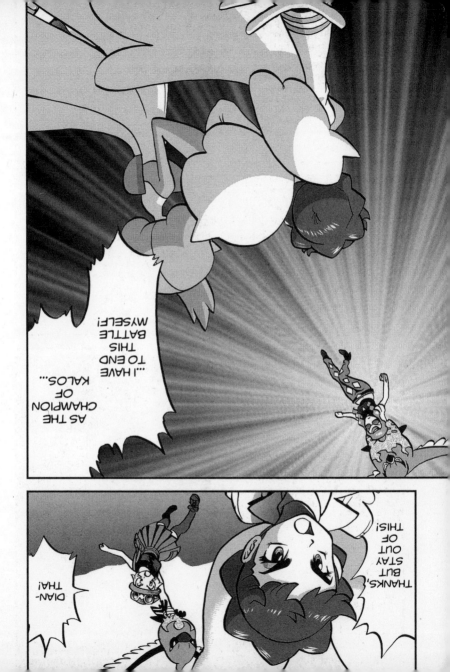

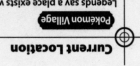

Current Location

Pokémon Village

Legends say a place exists where Pokémon live in hiding, but no one has ever found it.

Pokémon X • Y
Volume 11
Perfect Square Edition

Story by HIDENORI KUSAKA
Art by SATOSHI YAMAMOTO

©2017 The Pokémon Company International.
©1995-2017 Nintendo/Creatures Inc./GAME FREAK inc.
TM, ®, and character names are trademarks of Nintendo.
POCKET MONSTERS SPECIAL X•Y Vol. 6
by Hidenori KUSAKA, Satoshi YAMAMOTO
© 2014 Hidenori KUSAKA, Satoshi YAMAMOTO

Original Japanese edition published by SHOGAKUKAN.
English translation rights in the United States of America, Canada, the United
Kingdom, Ireland, Australia, New Zealand and India arranged with SHOGAKUKAN.

English Adaptation—Bryant Turnage
Translation—Tetsuichiro Miyaki
Touch-up & Lettering—Annaliese Christman
Design—Alice Lewis
Editor—Annette Roman

Printed in the U.S.A.

Published by
VIZ Media, LLC
P.O. Box 77010
San Francisco, CA 94107

10 9 8 7 6 5 4 3 2 1
First printing, July 2017

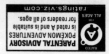

www.viz.com

www.perfectsquare.com

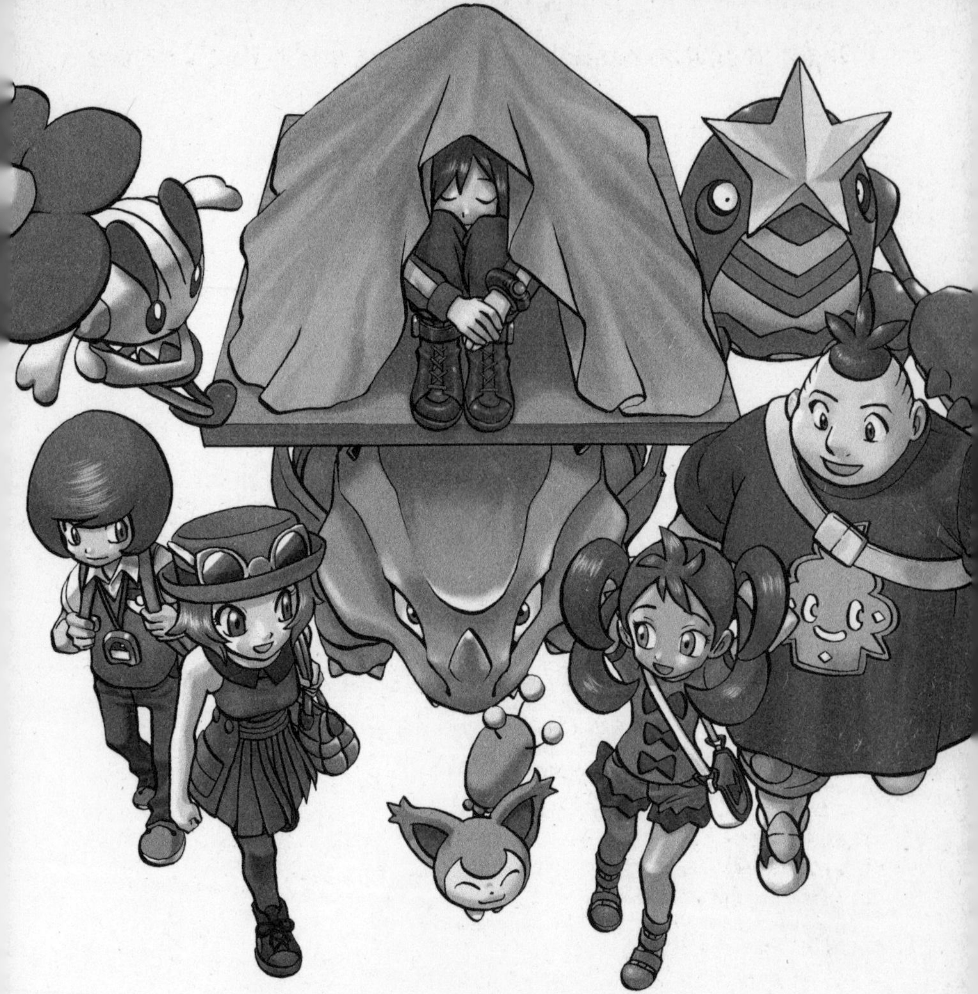

Team Flare is making a second attempt to activate the Ultimate Weapon and destroy the Kalos region! And this time, X, Y and friends will need some truly expert help to put a stop to their nefarious plan and heartless methods. Then our friends are faced with a moral dilemma...

Also, will Yveltal and Xerneas fight for eternity...?

VOLUME 12 AVAILABLE OCTOBER 2017!

FINAL VOLUME!

Begin your Pokémon Adventure here in the Kanto region!

RED & BLUE BOX SET

Story by HIDENORI KUSAKA   Art by MATO

Includes **POKÉMON ADVENTURES** Vols. 1-7 and a collectible poster!

All your favorite Pokémon game characters jump out of the screen into the pages of this action-packed manga!

Red doesn't just want to train Pokémon, he wants to be their friend too. Bulbasaur and Poliwhirl seem game. But independent Pikachu won't be so easy to win over!

And watch out for Team Rocket, Red... They only want to be your enemy!

Start the adventure today!

VIZ media
www.viz.com

PERFECT SQUARE

POKÉMON ADVENTURES
HEARTGOLD & SOULSILVER

Story by **HIDENORI KUSAKA**
Art by **SATOSHI YAMAMOTO**

In this **two-volume** thriller, troublemaker Gold and feisty Silver must team up again to find their old enemy Lance and the Legendary Pokémon Arceus!

Available now!

viz media
www.viz.com

PERFECT SQUARE

www.viz.com

POKÉMON^{TM}

POCKET COMICS

STORY & ART BY SANTA HARUKAZE

BLACK & WHITE
$9.99 US / $10.99 CAN

LEGENDARY POKÉMON
$9.99 US / $10.99 CAN

X•Y
$12.99 US / $13.99 CAN

A Pokémon pocket-sized book chock-full of four-panel gags, Pokémon trivia and fun quizzes based on the characters you know and love!

The adventure continues in the Johto region!

Pokémon™

ADVENTURES
GOLD & SILVER BOX SET

Includes
**POKÉMON
ADVENTURES**
Vols. 8-14
and a collectible
poster!

Story by
HIDENORI KUSAKA

Art by
**MATO,
SATOSHI YAMAMOTO**

More exciting Pokémon adventures starring Gold and his rival Silver! First someone steals Gold's backpack full of Poké Balls (and Pokémon!). Then someone steals Prof. Elm's Totodile. Can Gold catch the thief—or thieves?!

Keep an eye on Team Rocket, Gold... Could they be behind this crime wave?